DATE DUE		
APR 24 '95 DEC 05 00		
MAY 23 '95		
JUN 7 '95		
JUL 5 '95		
JUL 17 '95		
OCT 24 '95		
DEC 19 '95		
JAN 04 '96		
FEB 29 '96		
DEC 27 '97		
AUG 18 '98		
SEP 18 00		

BELOVED MOTHER
THE STORY OF NANCY WARD

Charlotte Jane Ellington

The Overmountain Press
JOHNSON CITY, TENNESSEE

To the Cherokee

Special Acknowledgments

The speeches from the treaty meetings and the council meetings, the letters from the Cherokee chiefs to the white officials, the deed stating the boundaries of Nancy Ward's property, and the message sent to the Cherokee Council meeting by Nancy Ward were adapted from those found in *Nancy Ward, Cherokee Chieftainess and Dragging Canoe, Cherokee-Chickamauga War Chief* by Pat Alderman; The Overmountain Press, P. O. Box 1261, Johnson City, Tennessee 37605.

The myths (with the exception of the Star Woman myth) and the shamanistic formulas were adapted from *Myths of the Cherokee and Sacred Formulas of the Cherokees* by James Mooney; Charles and Randy Elder—Booksellers, Publishers, Nashville, Tennessee, 2115 Elliston Place, Nashville, Tennessee 37203.

The Star Woman myth was adapted from *Voices of our Ancestors: Cherokee Teachings from the Wisdom Fire* by Dhyani Ywahoo; Shambhala Publications, 300 Massachusetts Avenue, Boston, Massachusetts 02115. It is printed in adapted form here by arrangement with Shambhala.

The vision of the three Cherokee reported at the council meeting at Oostanaula was adapted from *Trail of Tears: The Rise and Fall of the Cherokee Nation* by John Ehle; Anchor Books, Doubleday, 666 Fifth Avenue, New York, New York 10103.

For more detailed information check the "Notes" and the "Resources, Acknowledgments, Suggestions for Further Reading" sections in the back of the book.

Table of Contents

Approximate Location of Important Sites vi

Introduction..vii

People, Places, Terms ix

CHAPTER 1 - The Day We Awaited the Arrival of Five Killer.........1

CHAPTER 2 - How I Came to Live with Beloved Mother..............10

CHAPTER 3 - The Telling of the Stories 15

CHAPTER 4 - The Birth of Beloved Mother 19

CHAPTER 5 - How Wild Rose Came to be Called Nanyehi 22

CHAPTER 6 - Dragging Canoe and Attakullakulla......................31

CHAPTER 7 - The Ball Play and the Marriage............................39

CHAPTER 8 - The Battle of Taliwa 51

CHAPTER 9 - Ghigau 58

CHAPTER 10 - How Nanyehi Came to Marry Bryant Ward...........69

CHAPTER 11 - How the War with the Unakas Began...................77

CHAPTER 12 - The Way of the Wolf 88

CHAPTER 13 - The Voice of Dragging Canoe 93

CHAPTER 14 - The Words of Warning 97

CHAPTER 15 - The Rescue of Lydia Bean.................................106

CHAPTER 16 - "Their Cry Is for More Land" 116

CHAPTER 17 - "Our Cry Is All for Peace" 120

CHAPTER 18 - The Time When the Children Came....................129

CHAPTER 19 - The Treaty of Hopewell.....................................134

CHAPTER 20 - The Days of Chaos 138

CHAPTER 21 - The Arrival of Five Killer 147

CHAPTER 22 - The Day after Five Killer Came..........................158

CHAPTER 23 - The Time We Awaited the News
                of the Council Meeting....................................170

CHAPTER 24 - The Dancing of the Leaves................................177

Epilogue 182

Notes 183

Resources, Acknowledgments, Suggestions for Further Reading ..186

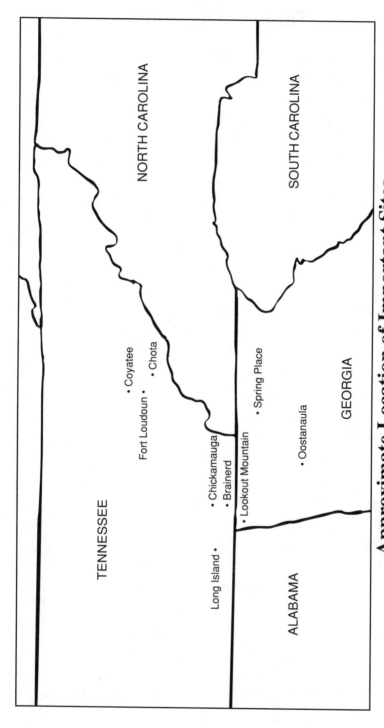

Approximate Location of Important Sites

The places are shown within the boundries of twentieth century state lines to give the modern-day reader an appreciation of locale.

Introduction

Beloved Mother is the story of Nancy Ward, a Cherokee chieftainess who lived from 1738 to 1822. The story is told through the voice of Dancing Leaf, a fictional, adopted daughter.

In writing this book, it was my intention to remain true to the commonly accepted facts and legends surrounding Nancy Ward's life. For this information I am indebted to a number of books, magazine articles, and newspaper clippings. I have detailed these resources in an appendixed section of this book.

It was also my desire to portray an authentic picture of Cherokee life during this time period. Woven into the story are Cherokee myths, shamanistic rituals and formulas, ceremonial events, and various everyday practices. The actual historical events of the Cherokee-White wars provide much of the framework of the novel. The speeches of the Indians and white men at the council meetings are edited, adapted versions of documented records of those meetings. Again—my sources for this information are listed in the appendix of the book.

Although facts and legends form the basic outline of the novel, there is much that is unknown about Nancy Ward. While writing this work, I found certain questions arising in my mind. What were her thoughts and feelings? What was her motive for action? Why was she so loved and respected by both the white people and her own people? What was her source of strength and power? For the answers to these questions, I had to rely on my imagination, and thus the fictional nature of the work. It is a work which, I hope, remains true to the character and spirit of Nancy Ward.

In addition, questions of a more universal nature also came to mind: How does one know one's place in this world? What is the relationship a people have to themselves, to other races, to the world about them, and to their concept of the Ruling Wisdom of the Universe? How is it that one deals with the polarities in life—war and peace, love and hate, birth and death?

I think it wise to point out that the novel is not, by any means, a complete account of Cherokee history during this time period. I have had to be selective with events covered. In some cases I have taken liberties with the actual time line of events to create a more tightly knit story. Also, I often found myself presented with varying and sometimes conflicting stories about the events and characters, and I selected those in keeping with the character development and themes presented here. The spelling of names and places was also a matter of choice, on occasion, for I found varying spellings in reference material.

I would like to thank all those who have given me encouragement in my pursuit of this endeavor—my husband, Ed; the members of Chap Reaver's winter 1992 writing class in Marietta, Georgia; Faye Taylor, librarian in Cleveland, Tennessee; my friends—Lynn Reinert, Peggy Mulkay, Eva Ingman, Mary Lou Bruder, and Jo Ann Chenot; Alison Jester, whose enthusiasm for my first chapter renewed my confidence. Thanks also to my publisher—the people of The Overmountain Press, whose faith in my work brought this project to completion.

And thanks to the Cherokee. My life has been enriched by my study of their culture. I hope that *Beloved Mother* will be a fitting tribute to them.

People, Places, Terms

Adawehi–shaman; medicine man

Ani-Yunwiya–the Principal People, the name the Cherokee gave to themselves

Attakullakulla–the great peace chief of the Cherokee; brother of Tame Doe; uncle to Nancy Ward; father of Dragging Canoe. His name means "Little Carpenter," which came from his ability to "carve out" treaties. He was a man of small stature, but he commanded the respect of both the Cherokee and the white people.

Lydia Bean–white woman rescued from burning at the stake by Nancy Ward

Beloved Mother–Nancy Ward, born 1738, died 1822. As a child she was called Wild Rose. Later she was called Nanyehi–one who is with the Nunnehi, the Spirit People. She attained the position of Beloved Woman, Ghigau, in the Cherokee tribe. She was called Nancy by the white traders and attained the surname Ward when she married Bryant Ward.

Betsy–Elizabeth; Nancy Ward's daughter by Bryant Ward

Billy–black slave; son of Oni and Tomi

Blue Lake–young companion of Five Killer. His mother was Cherokee, his father American.

Catherine–Nancy Ward's first child; a daughter born to her and Kingfisher

Chickamauga–Dragging Canoe moved his forces to this town and there set up his own council.

Chota–home and birthplace of Nancy Ward. It was considered one of the "mother towns" of the Cherokee nation. It was also considered a city of refuge where offenders of Cherokee law would not be prosecuted.

Dancing Leaf–adopted daughter of Nancy Ward. She was originally called Falling Leaf. She is the narrator of the story.

Dragging Canoe–cousin to Nancy Ward; son of Attakullakulla

Five Killer–Nancy Ward's son by her first marriage to Kingfisher. His first name was Short Fellow. He later attained the name of Five Killer when he distinguished himself as a warrior.

Fort Loudoun–British fort attacked by Cherokee

Hanging Maw–served as Principal Chief after the deaths of Oconostota and Attakullakulla

Kingfisher–Nancy Ward's first husband, a full-blood Cherokee

Lame Deer–the adawehi; shaman or medicine man

Long Fellow–Nancy Ward's brother

Colonel Joseph Martin–appointed agent to the Cherokee. He married Betsy (Elizabeth) Ward, Nancy's daughter by Bryant.

The Nunnehi–the Immortal Spirit People of the Mountain who reveal their presence only on certain occasions to the Cherokee

Oconostota–the great war chief of the Cherokee

Oni–black slave given to Nancy Ward by Bryant. She became Tomi's wife.

Spring Place–a mission school run by white men and attended by Dancing Leaf

Sudi–black slave; daughter of Oni and Tomi

Taliwa–important battle site where the Cherokee succeeded in pushing the Creeks further south

Tame Doe–mother of Nancy Ward

The Tassel–chief who presided at many peace conferences with the white men; also referred to as Corn Tassel and Old Tassel in reference books.

*_Tomi_–black slave awarded to Nancy Ward for her leadership in the Battle of Taliwa

Unaka–Cherokee term for the white man

Bryant Ward–a white trader; Nancy Ward's second husband

*These are fictional characters or fictional names given to characters who were thought to be a part of Nancy Ward's life. The other characters listed here are documented figures in Nancy Ward's life.

CHAPTER 1
The Day We Awaited
the Arrival of Five Killer

I remember well the day that I knew that I would write the story of Beloved Mother. It was the day that we awaited the arrival of her son, Five Killer. He was to arrive in the late afternoon, and it was he who would carry the message to the council meeting.

I, myself, had prepared the message, for it had been a full year that I had been learning the way of the "talking leaves" of the white people. It was Beloved Mother who had insisted that I do so.

"You will learn to read and write, Dancing Leaf," she said. "You are not so good at things with your hands. See?" she said as she held up the basket. "Your basket leans to one side and you take too long. The bottom of the basket is beginning to rot before you have finished the top. I have watched as you work. You start and you stop too often, and your thoughts are always elsewhere."

I could not look up as Beloved Mother was talking to me. Of course I knew I was no good at these things, as did everyone else. The other mothers often scolded me. My corn was never pounded small enough and was too chunky for the breads; it could only be used for the soups. And there had been the time when I was left to tend the simmering pot and I became distracted and forgot to add the water. The corn and meat had all cooked dry until there was only the black mush in the bottom. Even the cooking pot had to be thrown aside.

Until the moment with the basket, Mother had never said anything. I think she had pretended not to notice. On that day she noticed, though, and she noticed also my pain. She leaned forward as if to whisper a secret.

"I will tell you this, but you must not tell anyone, especially my own daughters or granddaughters.

"I, myself, was not so good with the work of the women. My own grandmother teased me and called me 'Pot Breaker,' because I was never able to make a clay pot without cracking it. I much preferred to spend my time hunting or at the ball play with the boys."

At these words my eyes grew wide, and I looked first at Beloved Mother and then at all about me.

"So how is it you have done so well?" I asked, for Beloved Mother was a great and respected woman. Everyone came to ask advice of her. Her house was never wanting for anything. When others were starving or in need of clothing, it was Beloved Mother who had more than enough to spare.

"I learned to put my efforts into the things that I do best. There are plenty of others who would do the other things. You will be unhappy if you do not do in this world the things that you do well. I have thought on this, and put my prayers to the fire in the evenings, that they might be carried with the smoke to the Elder Spirits above; and it is thus that it has come to me—you are good with words and thought. I have seen how you have fingered the books of my grandchildren and how you have marveled at the way the Unakas read from their papers. So it will be—you will learn the way of the talking leaves."

It was arranged that I go to the mission school at Spring Place. At first I was embarrassed because I was the only student with so many years. I was nearly fourteen, and the others were all under twelve. But I learned quickly, and soon it was I who was helping the smaller ones.

Beloved Mother would have preferred to go to the council meeting herself and there address the chiefs and warriors. Even when her daughter Betsy and her son-in-law Colonel Martin pleaded with her not to because of the spring floods, still she insisted she would go. It was only by the talk of her brother, Long Fellow, that she was discouraged.

"Sister," Long Fellow counseled, "your daughter's husband informs me that the rains have caused the rivers to be swollen so that the horses themselves have difficulty in crossing. You would not be able to ride comfortably in the horse-drawn cart. You would be forced to travel on horseback. I could not go that distance any more under such conditions, nor could you. Besides, you are needed here to supervise the business of the trading. There is wisdom in knowing how to best serve your people. Is this not so?"

So Beloved Mother agreed to stay. But she busied herself in talking with the women, and it was the Women's Council that decided that she would send a message if her son, Five Killer, would deliver it.

I had risen early on the day Five Killer would arrive, for there was much to do. There was food to be prepared for the evening meal and for the journey ahead, and I wanted to make one final copy of the message that would be in my best writing. So it was that I was annoyed when the Unaka boy from the white settlement came riding in. He came up the front steps of the porch with the loud, heavy walk. I knew before I saw his face it was not one of our people—he had the heavy footstep of the Unaka even though he was not a full man yet. It was Long Fellow who said that the Unaka has never learned the proper way to walk. He puts his foot down heavily, bringing the heel down first. The Indian walks softly, toe to heel, so as not to alert others to his presence, thus he has always been the superior hunter.

As if the loud walking were not enough, the Unaka then called out, "Granny! Granny Ward! Are you home? This is Jonathan Young. Ma sent me. She wants you to look at my hand! Are you there, Granny?"

Quickly I went to the porch, "Hush! She is still sleeping."

"But morning's half over," he protested, looking at the sky.

"She can sleep if she wants. She was up most of the night."

It was then that we heard the sound of Mother coughing. We both turned to look at the closed door, and we listened as she coughed.

"Is she gonna die?" asked Jonathan. "My granny sounded like that when she was old, and then after she had a bad spell one Sunday, she just died."

"No! She is not going to die! She will soon be well. It is because of the spring rains and the dampness in the air. See? Today the sun is out, and soon all things will dry up, and so will her cough, and she will be well! You will see. But now she needs her rest, so you will have to come back another day."

"I don't know. Ma said this was pretty serious and I wasn't to come home unless I had a remedy from Granny."

"Do not call her 'Granny!'" I stomped my foot as I said that. I did not like that name. All of the white settlers called her that, but I did not think that it sounded like a title of respect.

"Well, what do you call her?"

"I call her 'Beloved Mother' because she is my mother and she is a 'Beloved Woman' of our tribe."

"Isn't she awful old to be your mother?"

"I have been adopted by her. My own family was killed by the Unakas."

I gave him a look with the narrow eyes when I said that, but it did not bother him. He only said, "Plenty of white folks been kilt by Indians."

He bent down then and brushed a bug from his pant leg. When he had straightened up, he looked at me again and said, "Well, what does everyone else call her?"

"Our people call her 'Beloved Woman,' which is a title of great importance."

"Well, I dunno, Dancing Leaf. I don't fancy myself coming up on the porch and hollerin' out, 'Beloved Woman!'"

He looked at me for a moment. I said nothing, but continued to look at him with narrow eyes until finally he said, "Beloved Woman, huh? How do you say that in Cherokee? Maybe it sounds better that way."

"It is 'Ghigau,' and it is not to be hollered, no matter how you say it."

"Ghigau? Well, I can't fancy myself sayin' that either. Isn't 'Granny' close enough? They both begin with the same sound."

I would have told him no, but then it was Beloved Mother's voice that we both heard from behind us on the porch.

"Welcome, Jon Young. How is your mother and the new baby?"

"They're just fine, Granny. They're getting on real good. But it's me that's needin' a remedy. Ma sent me here so you could take a look at my hand."

"Well, come up here and let us see. What did you do?"

"See, I shot this coon that'd been gettin' in the corn shack. And I thought I'd shot him dead, but when I went to pick him up by the tail, he reached around and bit me."

"Hmmm. The coon can bite mean, and he can bite deep."

I looked at his hand as Mother held it in her own. The skin had swollen so that you could not see the marks of the bite, but you saw the redness of the angry skin and the oozing from under the crusted places.

"I don't think it is bad. I will give you a root that you must crush and mash and then mix with a small part of boiled water. You must put it on twice a day and wrap it with a clean cloth. You wait here. I will get it."

I looked at the Unaka as he waited, but I did not offer my thoughts, which is just as well, for they would have been "Why do you not learn to take care of these things yourself? Then you would not have to bother Beloved Mother, who has enough to worry about."

The Unaka voiced his own thoughts, though. "I sure hope Granny Ward gets over that cough and doesn't die, 'cause I don't know who could do the doctorin' for us then."

At this I said nothing, but stomped into the cabin, walking heel to toe like the Unakas. I did not come out to say good-by or to wish him well as he mounted his horse.

Beloved Mother came in after he left. "What was the talk between you and Jonathan? I could not hear the words, but only the sound of your voice. It sounded like the voice of an angry one. Why would you be angry with him? He is a polite child."

"He is not a polite child! He calls you 'Granny.'"

"And what is not polite about that? All of the people from the settlement call me 'Granny.' It is what the Unaka children call their grandmother. You will not be so rude to that one again."

I would have made another answer, but then we heard a voice from the yard in front of the house. It was a strange voice. At first I thought it was an animal or maybe a person sick or in mourning.

Mother opened the door and looked out.

"It is Lame Deer!" she exclaimed. "What is his purpose?"

It was then that Lame Deer, the adawehi, called out to her, answering her very question.

"Greetings, Beloved Woman. I have heard of your suffering, and I have come prepared to deliver you from it."

"And what suffering would that be? I am going well these days. Was it my brother who spoke with you? Long Fellow himself cannot make it a day without complaining of his ailments."

I remained silent and let the adawehi continue.

"It is said the Crippler is upon you, Ghigau. Where is the pain? In your knees, in your elbows, in your hips? Is it everywhere? Come. Already I prepare the formula. I will drive this intruder out."

Mother looked to the house and then out to the distance. She did this several times as if in confusion. I knew that she was thinking of all the things that had to be done before the arrival of Five Killer. I myself wished the adawehi would not have come on this day. True, it was I who had spoken to him of the condition of my mother, for I was worried. Beloved Mother did not go up and down the steps on the porch so easily. When she arose, it was only after walking about that her back was straight. Sometimes I would see her rubbing the root paste into her elbows and knees. Often I heard her moaning in her sleep. Still, I did not think that the adawehi would come on this day. It had been over a week since I had talked to him. Why had he not come earlier?

I could see that Beloved Mother was upset by his presence, but I knew she would think it rude to ask him to leave, for already he had constructed a fire, and even now was boiling the water. He had the terrapin shell out and the white beads and had proceeded to mutter over them.

"Very well," she said to him. "Let me give instructions to my daughter and the servants. And let us not waste time in the ceremony, Lame Deer, for I have much to do."

Then she called me aside. "Tell Sudi we will have venison for supper and sweet potatoes and corn and even fresh strawberries. And see that Sudi sweeps the cabin. Long Fellow will instruct Billy. They will need to shoot a deer."

It was good that we had Sudi and Billy, the black slaves, to help with the work, because Long Fellow and Beloved Mother were now both old, and I myself was at school most of the time.

The morning went quickly. Billy went with Long Fellow to shoot a deer. Beloved Mother knew that Five Killer would not eat the meat of the cow or the pig, for he believed, like many of our people, that such a meat would make one tired and lazy. Billy could have gone for the deer himself, but Long Fellow went along to make the proper petition to the spirit of the deer, for the old laws say that not to do so would upset the balance of life and death and offend the deer spirits, who would then cause a misfortune to the family.

The work of the adawehi was the work of the entire morning. I listened from the front porch as I churned the butter and mashed the corn for chowder.

Lame Deer began by calling forth the Red Spirit Dog of the East.

"Listen! Ha! In the Sun Land you repose, O Red Dog. Now you have swiftly drawn near to listen."

Then he called forth the Blue Dog of the North.

"Listen! Ha! From the Ice Land you have come, O Blue Dog. O Great One, you never fail in anything. You are now come to remove the intruder."

He called the Black Dog from the West.

"Listen! Ha! In the Dark Land you reign, O Black Dog. O Great One, appear and draw near running, for your prey never escapes."

He called the White Dog from the South.

"Listen! Ha! On the mountain of Wahala you repose, O White Dog. Oh, now you have swiftly drawn near to hear my call."

Then he addressed all four of the spirit dogs.

"O Great Spirits, you have never failed in anything! Ha! It is for you to loosen the bones. Relief is accomplished!"

The adawehi then took some of the mixture from the terrapin shell and rubbed it into the joints of Beloved Mother. The ceremony was repeated from the start three times that morning.

When all was finished, Beloved Mother presented Lame Deer with a deer hide.

"Many thanks, Lame Deer. The deerskin I give you will insure that your words are heard and that your medicine is strong."

We watched as Lame Deer gathered his things and put them in his pouch and began the walk to the village. Mother turned to me then.

"If the adawehi comes again, you will tell him that I have journeyed to visit my daughter. I will speak to Long Fellow about this."

She then walked toward the house, but when she was at the door, she turned and looked at me. I could see that the thought had just entered her mind that it was I who had sent for the adawehi. But I pretended that I noticed nothing, and I mounted the stairs and said to her, "You will rest this afternoon. All will be ready. I will sit by you as you nap, and I will finish copying the letter."

I helped her to lie down and went to get my paper and pen. When

I returned, already she was asleep. The words of the Unaka boy then echoed in my mind: "Is Granny gonna die?"

The last few months I had been afraid of this very thing. That is why I did not return to school during the planting season. I knew that I must take care of her. I would see that she would get her rest and would eat the proper food. I wanted her to become well again and to take charge of all things as she did before.

I knew of no life without Beloved Mother. It is true that I once had another life, but it was before I could remember. I could not bear to think of life without her.

I worked on the copy of the message and listened to her breathe. She looked small on her mat, and her breath did not come evenly.

It was then that I vowed to write the story of Beloved Mother. I would put the stories from her life on the pages of the talking leaves, and this would be something I could keep forever.

CHAPTER 2
How I Came to Live with Beloved Mother

I myself came to live with Beloved Mother ten summers ago when I was a child of five. Until then, I had lived with my mother and my brother and my grandparents. These things I know because they had been told to me by Spotted Deer and Lame Beaver and other survivors of our village. I do not remember this other life. It is gone from me.

I remember only sitting amidst the bushes on the banks of a flowing stream. I knew that I could not leave that place; my mother had put me there and told me not to leave, no matter what I heard. From the distance I heard noises—loud, unpleasant noises. So unpleasant that I sat for a long while with my hands pushing tightly over my ears. I wanted badly to run away from that place, but I knew I could not leave. I had to stay there in the bushes by the stream.

The day went and the night came and I grew cold. But still I tried to make no sound, and I stayed in that same place. I rested my back against the bushes and dozed and awoke all through the night. The next morning, I was wakened by the sound of voices. Horses with riders were wading the stream. I could tell from their voices that they were Ani-Yunwiya. I knew then I could sit in this place no longer. Slowly I stood up. It was then that the horses reared up and the warriors drew their rifles and pointed them at me. But this did not frighten me, for my feelings were numbed, even as my arms and legs were numbed from the cold night air.

I did not recognize the men; they were not of our village. The short one called to the other two: "Look! It is only a little girl! We have found another that has survived!"

The warrior jumped from his horse and came slowly toward me.

"Do not be afraid. We will help you. You will be safe with us. Are there any more with you?"

I shook my head.

"Where are your parents? Your grandparents?"

Again I shook my head.

I could understand these words, but I could not make any words of my own, nor did I know the answer to his questions. My mind was a great blank space—I knew nothing. I did not know of parents or grandparents or sisters or brothers or other people. I knew of no village either.

"No matter, little one," the warrior said. "I will take you to a place where it is safe and warm and you can have good things to eat. Our camp is only a little way from here."

The warrior put me on the back of his horse and took me to the camp. There were other warriors there and several people from my village.

The next day, we began the journey to the place the warriors called home. It was a long journey. Five times we saw the sun rise and set. On the sixth sunrise we crossed a river and rode up a small hill. There we saw the settlement. It was a large settlement, much larger than my own.

The warrior took me to a dwelling at the edge of the town, near the river. Such a dwelling I had never seen before. It was a large cabin, and the rows of logs were cut so that they fit together at the corners.

It was Beloved Mother who came to the door, and it was her son, Five Killer, who brought me there.

"She is only one of six brought back from the village," said Five Killer. "The others are all dead or have taken refuge in the mountains. We could find no more. She has not spoken since we first found her, but we are told she is called Falling Leaf."

"Welcome," Beloved Mother said as she kneeled down and looked into my face. "This will be your home now. You will be as one of us. Go now with this one—Tall Girl. She will show you where you may sleep."

Tall Girl and I walked around to the back of the cabin, where four or five other children were playing. Then we entered another large dwelling, where I saw many sleeping mats.

"You can sleep next to me," said Tall Girl. "Did you bring your sleeping mat?"

I said nothing, but only looked down.

"No matter. We will find you one. You may not be here long, you know. Many of us leave and go live with other mothers or fathers or grandparents of the village. You are small. You will need a family."

This I knew was a good place, a safe place. There was plenty of food. There were mothers and fathers and grandparents. There were other children. But as I went about with the other children during the day, my mind remained a great blank. I could see and hear the others, but yet I felt that a great cloud surrounded me so that I was not really in their world. I did not talk with the others, but only followed them about as they gathered wood and helped with the cooking and the matters of basket and pottery making. Nor did I join them in the playing of the games.

I came to dread the nighttime, when the others had all fallen asleep, and only the embers of the fire remained. That is when the loud noises came again. They would become louder and louder until finally I would sit up and put my hands over my ears and rock back and forth. Tall Girl would wake up then and try to reason with me.

"What is wrong? Why do you put your hands over your ears? There is nothing out there. I hear nothing. Go back to sleep!"

But I did not often go back to sleep. Tall Girl became annoyed and complained to Beloved Mother.

"I cannot sleep next to this one. She wakes up every night and rocks and mutters things I cannot understand."

That is when Beloved Mother brought me into her own cabin

and put my mat beside hers. I was glad to sleep there, but I was afraid that I would disturb her and she would be angry if I awoke in the night. And yet I could not help myself. Again at night, when I was nearly asleep, the noises began. I had to stop them! I could not restrain my actions. I sat up and covered my ears and closed my eyes and began to rock back and forth. It was not long until I noticed that there was a pair of arms around mine and a pair of hands over mine and a body cradled around mine. We were as one, and we slowly rocked back and forth. Gently I rocked with Mother until the noises stopped. When they stopped, I did not know exactly, but I awoke late the next morning, after the others had all risen and were already gathering firewood. I knew then that I had been asleep for many hours.

Never again did I hear the noises in my sleep. But I continued to sleep in the same house as Beloved Mother, even as I do today.

At this time I still did not talk though. The words did not come. They did not come for some time after that—not until the time of year of changing colors and falling leaves. I remember well that certain day when four of us children set out to gather nuts and berries. As we entered the meadow and looked to the valley and the mountains in the distance, we were suddenly seized with a burst of joy, and we skipped our way into the woods. We filled the first basket with berries and then gave it to younger brother, who was too small to be of much help and could only serve by holding on to things. Then we raced off to gather nuts, and we scolded back to the squirrels who scolded us from overhead. When our baskets were full, we turned to see that little brother had eaten most of the berries.

"What happened to the berries?" Tall Girl asked him.

"A bear came and took them away from me. A big black bear."

At this we all burst into laughter, for his mouth and fingers were stained with the blue-purple of the berries. We laughed so hard that we rolled upon the ground. It was the first time I had laughed since I had come to this place. When finally we had quieted down, I looked up and saw the colored leaves above, dancing in the wind. Some of them dropped from the tree and twirled to the ground below. It seemed as if they had put on their best attire and colored themselves with the red vermillion as do the dancers in our ceremonies. And suddenly I wanted to join them. I arose and began to dance also in small, twirling circles. Then I raised my hands above my head and danced in larger circles and sang a song to the dancing leaves. I felt light and free and full of joy to be a part of all of this.

The other two girls, Tall Girl and Smiling Eyes, stopped laughing and turned to watch me with rounded eyes and open mouths. Tall Girl ran back toward the cabin and came back with Beloved Mother.

"See, Mother. She dances and sings like a crazy old woman."

Beloved Mother looked at me and asked, "Falling Leaf, what is it you do?"

I laughed and shouted to her, "Mother, I am dancing with the leaves."

Mother watched me for a moment, then she, too, began laughing and dancing, and she called to the other children.

"She is not crazy. She is only dancing. Come. All of us—we will dance with her."

And so we were all dancing in the meadow and raising our arms to the sky above and shouting our greetings to the mountains in the distance. We danced until we fell exhausted into one heap in the meadow. Beloved Mother then said to me, "From now on, Falling Leaf, you will be called 'Dancing Leaf.'"

CHAPTER 3
The Telling of the Stories

It was soon after the day of dancing leaves that I was formally adopted by Beloved Mother. It was at the time of the Green Corn Festival, a time when the problems and misfortunes of the past are cast aside and all are brought into new life and harmony. At the Ceremony of New Names, Beloved Mother announced me as her daughter, Dancing Leaf, and presented me with the sleeping mat in which was woven the sign of the wolf, for I was now of the wolf clan as was Beloved Mother.

To be given a new name is a thing of great importance to the Ani-Yunwiya. On that evening, as we gathered at the council fire, the great storyteller, Long Arrow, recounted for us the story of our ancestors and how they came to have the name of Ani-Yunwiya.

I sat within the arms of Beloved Mother and listened to these words of Long Arrow. The fire burned brightly in the council square, and though Long Arrow's voice was low, it carried well and all could hear his words.

"We are the Ani-Yunwiya, the Principal People, who journeyed to this place from a great land to the north. Our ancestors came from a far distant country in search of a place where they might be safe from their enemies.

"Their journey was a perilous one. At one time they were beset with the deadliest of serpents. A great many of the people were killed, until their great leader, Wasi, shot the serpents with deadly arrows, and they were driven away, never to return. At another time, a period of terrible drought came upon them, and they nearly all perished for lack of water until Wasi found a beautiful spring which came from a rock. They came upon a great river then, and it seemed to be impassable, but they made a great bridge by tying together grapevines, and thus they crossed and traveled on.

"It was while they were on this great journey that they received the sacred fire of heaven. They were charged by the Elder Spirits above with the keeping of the knowledge of the fire, for it is the knowledge of the fire that contains the secret of the way of harmony of all things. This knowledge they were to keep for the benefit of all peoples, and thus we have called ourselves the Ani-Yunwiya, the Principal People, and the other peoples have called us the Cherokee, the keepers of the fire.

"Now this sacred fire was carried with them until they reached this land, and still it burns today in the sacred council houses of all of the beloved towns. It is this sacred fire which is rekindled every year at this time, the time of the Green Corn Festival."

Tall Girl then spoke. "Tell us, Long Arrow, the story of how it was in the early days, when the animals and plants could talk and lived in harmony with our people upon the land."

Long Arrow nodded and continued his narration.

"It is true that in the old days the animals—the birds, the fishes, the insects—they could all talk, and so could all the plants. This was the time when they lived as equals with our people in peace and friendship. But as time went on, the people multiplied and filled the earth faster than the animals, and soon they were crowding out the plants and animals. What is more, the people began to invent and use weapons against the animals—bows, knives, blowguns, spears, and hooks. They killed animals for their skins and their meat. The smaller creatures were stepped upon and crushed without so much as a thought.

"The animals then held counsel and decided to take revenge upon the people. The Deer agreed to send rheumatism to every hunter who would kill one of their own without first taking care to ask pardon. The Fishes and Reptiles decided that they would punish Man by making him dream of snakes that were twining about him or by having dreams of decaying fish. The other animals also devised various diseases with which to afflict Man.

"Now the Plants were sympathetic to Man. They agreed to help him. They devised a remedy for the diseases brought on by the Animals. Thus it was that medicine was born, and for every illness there is a remedy in the Plant world, if only we would know all of them."

Many stories were repeated by Long Arrow and other storytellers that night—how the world was made, how man got fire, what the stars are made of—for these are the stories that are always told at the time of our festivals.

When the time of storytelling had ended, Attakullakulla, the great peace chief, stood and announced to the people, "We will now depart, and our women will take an ember from the sacred fire that we may thus rekindle the light in our own homes."

I then went with Beloved Mother and the other women. We placed within our clay pot an ember from the fire and took it to our cabin and there relit our own fire.

Thus it was that I was a child in the town of Chota, and it was there that I learned the beloved stories of our people. Now I loved nothing more than I loved the telling of the stories. When the other children squirmed about or would wander off, always I would sit with folded legs and wide eyes, and it was I who would always beg for more stories.

Sometimes the other mothers and the older children would become annoyed with me, for while they were busy with their hands—making baskets, shaping pots, preparing hides—always I would be asking questions of them: "Do you know the story of how the buzzard's head is bald?" or "Tell us why the bullfrog's head is striped."

It was Catherine, Beloved Mother's oldest daughter, who was visiting at one time and who said to Beloved Mother, "This one wastes too much time with stories. She distracts us all, and our work is not soon enough finished."

But Beloved Mother took her aside, and although I was not supposed to hear, I heard the words she said:

"You must be patient with this one. Many of us have lived and grown up with our families and have heard their stories often repeated. But this one has lost her first family, and the stories have gone with them. She has no early history of her own, and she would seek to create one for herself in the telling of these stories. It is important to her. We must be patient with her."

Thus it was that Beloved Mother was always generous in the telling of the stories. And in the long evenings of the winter months, she would often tell me the stories from her own life—how she was born; how she listened to the stories of her grandmother and her uncle Attakullakulla, the great peace chief; how she became Beloved Woman of our people; and how she attended the great peace meetings with the Unaka chiefs.

CHAPTER 4
The Birth of Beloved Mother

The story of the birth of Beloved Mother was told to her by her own grandmother. Grandmother was present at the birth, and it was she who had arranged for the assistance of the adawehi, Lone Dove, for he was the most trusted adawehi in the birthing of the babies.

Now Tame Doe was the mother, and when her time had come, she went with Grandmother and Lone Dove to the birthing hut at the side of the river. In those days the mothers giving birth were always removed from the rest of the tribe and taken to a special place.

Grandmother was uneasy. It was Tame Doe's first child. She had been there already for half a day and all of the night, and still there was no child. At near sunrise the adawehi said to Grandmother, "This one does not want to leave the comfort of the womb. I will say the special formula that he might be persuaded."

Lone Dove then took powder from the yellow root and placed it on top of Tame Doe's head, and then upon her chest, and upon the palm of each hand. Then he began the chant:

Little brave, little brave,
Hurry, hurry!
Jump down! Jump down!
Little brave, hurry!
It's a bow! Come!
Let's see who'll get it!

Then the adawehi blew upon the yellow powder.

They waited until they saw the red of the sun in the eastern sky, but still nothing had happened.

"It must be a girl," the adawehi informed Grandmother. "We will repeat the procedure for a girl." Again he began the chant:

Little maiden! Little maiden!
Jump down! Jump down!
Little maiden, hurry!
It's a sifter! Come!
Let's see who'll get it!

It was at the point of full sunrise that Grandmother heard the cry of the newborn. It was an angry cry that protested being taken so rudely from the warmth of the mother's body. Grandmother was pleased to see that it was indeed a girl. She paused before the fire and gave thanks for the child's safe passage into the world, and it was then that the thought came to her that she herself would take the new one to water. She wrapped the baby carefully in a blanket, and quietly she left the hut.

The adawehi called after her, "Where do you go now?"

"I go to wash this one in the stream of life as is the custom of our people."

"But," protested the adawehi, "it is not asked of us to take the newborn to the water of the cold mountain stream. Here, I have brought some water. We will heat it first, and then we will wash this new one."

"This is the way it is to be, Lone Dove," Grandmother said, and she hurried down the path to the water's edge, leaving the adawehi to mutter at her insistence.

As she approached the stream, Grandmother saw that the mist was still rising from the water, for the morning sun had not yet reached this spot. Cautiously she waded into the water. The cold of the running stream was always a shock, but she was used to it, for it was the custom of our people to go to water every morning. She cupped her hand, drew some water, and gently poured it over the infant. The baby cried out and raised her fists and stretched her legs in protest. Grandmother dried her and wrapped her again in the blanket and drew her close. As she looked up from her task, she gasped, for she saw a sight she had never seen before—it was a white wolf.

Of course she had seen a wolf before, but never a white one. She knew the wolf to be a messenger from the spirit world. Many stories were told of how the wolf had come to the aid of warriors in battle or travelers on the road. A white animal was always considered sacred, so a white wolf must be a very special messenger indeed.

Softly she called to him, "Hail, Brother Wolf! I thank you for your presence. This one is a special one. I know you come to tell me this. I will take good care of her."

At these words the wolf arose and howled softly in reply and then turned and trotted into the woods.

Grandmother turned and hurried up the path. She thought, at first, to ask the adawehi the meaning of this occurrence, but she remembered then the words of the old people who had gone before: "It is bad luck to tell others of a meeting with a creature from the spirit world before the passing of seven days." So she said nothing, and when the seven days had passed, still she said nothing.

It was many years before Grandmother told of the meeting with the white wolf, and then it was only to Beloved Mother herself.

CHAPTER 5
How Wild Rose
Came to be Called Nanyehi

Beloved Mother was born into the wolf clan, the largest clan of the Ani-Yunwiya people. There are seven clans in all, as there are seven directions and seven festivals of the year, for seven is the sacred number of our people. The other clans are the Deer People, the Bird People, the Paint People, the Wild Potato People, the Long Hair People, and the Blue People.

It is believed that those of the wolf clan are blood brothers to the wolves of the mountain. The people of the wolf clan revere the wolf for his cunning and his strength and his endurance. It is the wolf who best adapts to the contours of the mountains and the swamps. It is the wolf who can survive the cold of the mountain nights without suffering from frostbite. It is forbidden of the Ani-Yunwiya to kill one of the brother wolves.

So it was that Beloved Mother remembered well the day when the Unaka trader killed the wolf and brought him to his home in the Cherokee village. Beloved Mother was only five years old at that time, and in those days she was called Wild Rose because her skin was the reddish color of the wild rose. But the time when the trader came with the wolf was the time when Beloved Mother acquired a new name and a new status among her people.

It was Trader John who came strolling through the village with the wolf strapped across his back. Wild Rose and the other children were the first to notice. They quickly gathered around him and followed him to his home.

Trader John approached his cabin and called to Smiling Face, his Cherokee wife, to come out to help skin the animal. Wild Rose and her friends knew, of course, the taboo against the killing of the wolf, and they were afraid of what would happen, so they hid behind the bushes.

Smiling Face came out, and when she saw the dead wolf she cried out, "Ai-Ye!" What have you done!" She ran quickly to find the elders of the village. When she returned, it was with two of the chiefs and the adawehi and a small group of warriors. Quickly the adawehi directed the warriors to carry the body of the wolf to the river, where the proper ceremony could be performed.

The children followed close behind, and soon a large crowd was attracted, until nearly the whole village was gathered at the river. The adawehi paid no notice, though, as he was intent upon his purpose. He quickly began the ceremony.

"O Brother Wolf, how unhappy we are to find your remains! It is not we, the Ani-Yunwiya, who have killed you. It is the ugly one, the Unaka. Do not send the game from us. We will, instead, send this one out, that your curse may follow him.

"Thank you, O Brother Wolf, for your kindness and protection. We will forever live by your guidance, and forever will we revere your tracks."

Then he took the gun which they had taken from the trader and held it up.

"This gun, O Brother Wolf, we have taken from the Unaka. We will cleanse it in the healing waters of Long Man, the River. Here it will be buried, and it will never be used again. This we do in honor of you, O Great Brother Wolf."

When Trader John realized that they meant to bury his gun in the river, he rushed at them crying, "Hey, I need that! Idiots! Give me back my gun!"

But quickly the warriors surrounded him, and the adawehi continued the ritual. Trader John turned then and angrily strode to his home. The children followed at a safe distance to see what would become of him next.

When he reached his dwelling, he found that his sleeping mat and his clothes and all of his belongings had been placed outside of his cabin.

"What is the meaning of this?" he demanded of his wife.

"You must leave. It is not good for you to be here anymore. We are no longer man and wife."

"Do not tell me, woman, where I must go and what I must do." And he tried to push past her and enter his cabin.

But the brothers of Smiling Face were close by and stepped forward and said, "You must leave. This house belongs to our sister. She has placed your things outside. You two have now split the blanket. You are no longer man and wife, and you, therefore, may not live among us."

The warriors decided to organize a party and to trail the Unaka to make sure that he did leave the village and that he did not return. They called to some of the young braves, inviting them to go along and to make a hunt of it while they were out.

When Wild Rose saw that some of the young warriors, including her cousin Dragging Canoe, were to go, she shouted to them, "Take me, too!"

"You cannot go, Wild Rose!" Dragging Canoe insisted. "You are too small."

And that was true, for Wild Rose was only five at the time. Still, she was determined, and when the men and boys had left, she followed them from a distance on foot. When she came to the stream, she did not know what to do, and she was afraid to cross, so she sat and thought about the hunger which was now gnawing at her stomach.

It was not long before she fell asleep. When she awoke, it was dark. She knew then she must spend the night at this place.

The next morning, she awoke to see two tall figures hovering over her. It was a man and a woman, and they appeared to be Ani-Yunwiya. The woman wore a deerskin skirt and vest and moccasins.

Her long hair was braided in the back and hung nearly to her knees. The man wore buckskin clothes also. His head was plucked bare except for a strip down the middle, the typical crown piece of the Ani-Yunwiya warrior.

Wild Rose could not avert her eyes from these two figures. She knew it was a matter of great rudeness to look upon them so, yet she felt drawn to them and could not look away. There was something different about them. What was it? She reached to touch the woman's hand. Yes, it was real flesh. At least she thought so, but there was something different about the feel of it. She tried to judge their age. They were not children, and they seemed too old for parents and too young to be grandparents.

"We will fix this one something to eat now," the woman said to the man. "You take her to catch a fish, and I will fix the corn bread."

The man took her by the hand and led her to the edge of the stream. He gave her a deep basket and told her to hold it sideways and he would scare a fish into it. Then he dove beneath the surface. He was under such a long time that Wild Rose thought to cry out for the woman to come. But then suddenly she felt a plop inside her basket, and she turned it up and lifted it to see a large catfish. At the same time, the man thrust his upper body from the water.

She and the man walked a short distance through the woods to the camp where the woman was preparing the corn bread. They cooked the fish over the fire, and quietly they ate their meal. There was very little said. There seemed to be no need to talk. They listened to the sounds of the morning. The squirrel above chattered, and a hawk circled overhead. As they watched, a young deer passed them on his way to the stream for a drink. He turned to look at them, and when he had judged them to be no threat, he continued on his way.

When the sun reached the middle of the sky, the man said, "We must be on our way."

They rose and began their trek through the woods. As they came over a low hill, Wild Rose recognized the bend of a certain pine tree.

She ran eagerly ahead because she knew that just over the hill she would find the stream that ran close to the village. And sure enough, it was so.

Breathless, she climbed upon a rock to await the arrival of the man and the woman. Looking ahead toward the camp, she could see the young braves who only yesterday refused to take her hunting. They were pointing at her and shouting back toward the village.

"It is Wild Rose. Right there! On the rock by the stream. Run! Tell Tame Doe and Grandmother we have found her."

Wild Rose turned to look back at the man and the woman. She saw that they had halted and had raised their hands in a farewell salute. Then they turned and disappeared into the woods.

Wild Rose called to them to stop and to come and meet her mother. But it seemed as if they had dissolved into the air, for one minute they were there and the next all she could see were the branches of the tree.

Dragging Canoe was there beside her demanding, "Where have you been? We have been looking all night! You want me to take you hunting when you play such games! I do not think one who plays in such a way is deserving of the hunt."

"No matter. I have already caught a fish and cooked him for my breakfast," Wild Rose answered, as if to say, "Who needs to be taken on a hunt?"

Dragging Canoe looked at her and laughed disbelievingly until she held up the fishing basket as proof.

"See?" she said. "This is how I caught him."

At this, Dragging Canoe seized the basket and turned it over and over in his hands.

It was then that Tame Doe, Wild Rose's mother, was there. She chided Wild Rose and hugged her at the same time. "Where have you been? Are you well? What did you do?" Then she scooped up her daughter and began carrying her back to the village.

Dragging Canoe called after her, "Mother," (for children call all mothers by the title "Mother") "she says she caught a fish with this basket."

"Is that so? And where did you get this basket, Wild Rose?"

"From the man and woman of the forest, Mother. We cooked the fish and ate the corn bread, and then they brought me here."

By then a crowd of the villagers had gathered around Wild Rose and Tame Doe.

Grandmother was there, too, and she asked, "What did they look like, this man and woman?"

"They were Ani-Yunwiya, but they do not live in the village," Wild Rose answered.

The people began to talk among themselves. They could not be Creek since the child had said they dressed and wore their hair in the manner of the Ani-Yunwiya. Chief Attakullakulla sent out a search party, but no trace of them could be found.

Tame Doe laughingly said, "This one! I would not be surprised if she were with the Nunnehi."

But the others did not laugh, and they talked among themselves. For several days they approached Tame Doe and demanded questions of Wild Rose.

"Did these people talk? Did they scare you? Did they take you to their house under the river?"

Finally Tame Doe said, "It is enough. Leave the child alone. She knows only that she was with a kind man and a kind woman, and they caught a fish. It is enough."

The incident had stirred the people of the village, though, and in the evenings when they gathered by the fires, they begged the old people to tell them the stories of the Nunnehi.

It was Attakullakulla, uncle of Wild Rose, who explained the knowledge of the Nunnehi.

"The Nunnehi," he began, "are the Immortal Spirit People of the Mountain. They live in the highlands, especially in the bald mountains, on the high peaks where no timber grows. They have large council houses in Pilot Knob and under the Nikwasi Mound to the east and another under Blood Mountain to the south. They are usually invisible; they reveal themselves to us only when they want to be seen.

"Their greatest love is music and dancing. Sometimes our hunters hear their drums beating and their songs being sung. When the hunters move closer to the sound to try to find its source, they find that the noise has shifted to a different direction, so that it is now behind them, or now it seems to be coming from a rock in the opposite direction. Never has a hunter been able to find the place where they live and dance and sing."

It was the old warrior, Laughing Song, who then told the following tale:

"The people of the village of Nottely know of the four Nunnehi women who came to a Green Corn Dance. Everyone thought they were visitors from a different settlement. At midnight they left to go home, and some of the men stepped outside of the council house to cool off and watched the women go down the trail to the river. Just as they came to the water, they disappeared. One minute they were there, plain and visible, and the next they were not, although the trail was plainly visible, and there was no place or no reason to hide."

Long Neck told the next story:

"In a place north of Blood Mountain, there is a hole in the ground. Clouds of vapor rise from the hole, and they warm the air around them. The old people have always said that the clouds are from the fires of the Nunnehi in the council houses under the mountain. Sometimes the hunters stop at this place and warm themselves, but they are afraid to stay for long."

Oconostota, the great warrior and chief, told of a town on the Little Tennessee River:

"The town of Nikwasi was saved by the Nunnehi. Once, a powerful tribe from the Southeast had come into the area. The warriors gathered the women and children into the council house and went out to fight the advancing tribe. They were soon overpowered and were starting to retreat when a stranger appeared among them and shouted to their chief, 'Call your men back and rest. We will take over the battle for you now and drive back this enemy.'

"The chief thought this warrior to be perhaps a chief from a neighboring village who had come to help, and he did as he was asked. As his warriors fell back to the trail, they saw a large troop of warriors coming from a mound. They came out by the hundreds and were all clearly visible to the warriors of the Ani-Yunwiya. But once they approached the battleground, they became invisible, and the enemy could not see the arrows or the tomahawks coming at them. The enemy tribe began to retreat. As they did, they tried to hide themselves behind trees and rocks, but the arrows of the Nun-nehi would go around the rocks and find them anyway. All of the warriors were killed except maybe six or so. The Nunnehi chief admonished the six because they had attacked a peaceful tribe who had done them no harm. He told them to return to their home and tell their people of these happenings."

The old woman, Corn Basket, told the legend of the Nunnehi who lived near the creek where Wild Rose was found by the two strangers:

"At one time there was another town of people who lived there. They prayed and fasted for seven days in honor of the Nunnehi. At the end of this time, the Nunnehi were pleased, and they took the entire village of people down under the water to live with them. You can hear them on a warm summer day if you are very still. Their voices rise from the river as they talk with one another. Our fishermen have had great luck there, especially with their dragnets, for our lost kinsmen below make sure that their fish-drags stop well and catch the fish, for these kinsmen of ours do not wish to be forgotten."

Thus it was that the people of the village of Chota became convinced that Wild Rose was found and brought back to the village by the Nunnehi. Thereafter they began to call her Nanyehi, which means "one who goes about with the Nunnehi." But Grandmother spoke sharply against this.

"Do not call her this! She will think she is one with the Immortals!"

Still, most of the village people from then on called her Nanyehi, and it was only Grandmother and Tame Doe who continued to call her Wild Rose.

CHAPTER 6
Dragging Canoe and Attakullakulla

It was Dragging Canoe, cousin of Nanyehi, who had refused to take her on the hunting trip and who had found her sitting on a rock the following day. When they were young, these two were often together, for Attakullakulla, the great peace chief, was father to Dragging Canoe, and he was also brother to Tame Doe, mother of Nanyehi.

Although Dragging Canoe was several years older than Nanyehi, the two were good friends. Nanyehi loved the hunt and the ball play, and she admired her older cousin, who did well at these things. And Dragging Canoe admired the fire spirit of his cousin, so he often took her hunting with a blowgun or fishing with a spear.

Now Dragging Canoe was not always called by this name. In fact, it was not long after the time when Mother was lost in the woods and took the name of Nanyehi that Dragging Canoe took his name. It was a time when the Cherokee planned a raid against the Shawnee. The warriors had fasted and purified themselves at the scratching ceremony. Dragging Canoe was determined that he would go also, although he was only ten years old.

Attakullakulla, his father, spoke to him sharply, "No! You do not go. The time is not yet right for you to go on these raids. You will stay behind and help to protect the women and children who are here."

Dragging Canoe said nothing, and on the morning the warriors left, he was there likewise to bid them farewell. As soon as they were out of sight, though, and the village people could no longer hear their war whoops, he returned to his dwelling and took up his bow and arrow. Nanyehi saw this and approached him, "Where do you go,

Cousin? Attakullakulla has told you to stay home."

"Do not bother me now, Nanyehi. Just as you were determined to go at one time on the hunt with me, so am I determined that I will go on the raid with the other warriors. I cannot take you with me. But you must stay behind and not tell Mother or Grandmother where I am until the sun is high in the sky. Do this for me, and I will bring you a present. I will give to you the first scalp that I take in the battle."

Nanyehi agreed. For three days she patiently awaited his return. She believed that he would indeed return with a scalp and in the position of an honored warrior.

On the evening of the fourth day, the people of the village heard the victory war cries of the returning warriors. As was the custom, the warriors and the people gathered around the fire to tell the stories of the successful raid.

It was the warrior Black Crow who recounted the story of Dragging Canoe:

"This one is our youngest warrior. He deserves special recognition on this day. Although his father forbade him, he was determined to show his ability to go to war. It was as we approached our canoes tied to the edge of the river that we came upon this one. We noticed that one of the canoes did not rock in the wind, and we judged it to be heavier than the others. We knew that someone was in it. Cautiously we approached, with our arrows drawn and our rifles pointed, for it could have been a Shawnee. But no, inside the canoe, hiding on the floor, was this one!

"Now his father thought to send him back with another warrior. But our braves counseled with Attakullakulla. 'Is he not courageous and persistent? Give him a chance.'

"Attakullakulla made then an official pronouncement: 'When a young brave can carry a canoe across the land to get from one navigable place in the river to the next, then that young brave is man enough to travel with our raiding warriors.'

"Attakullakulla thought that this would discourage his son. He expected that his son would return home. But as he turned his back and walked away, the other warriors called to him, 'Look, he is doing it! He is dragging the canoe! Look! He drags the canoe!' And indeed so great was this one's determination that he was dragging the canoe across the sandy banks.

"Attakullakulla then allowed his son to accompany the party of warriors. Such determination merits special recognition," Black Crow concluded.

Oconostota, the red war chief, then presented the young warrior with a wreath of swan feathers, the insignia of the fierce warrior. Oconostota turned to the people and announced, "This one, henceforth, will be known as 'Dragging Canoe.'"

Nanyehi was glad for her cousin that he had merited such attention, but she was annoyed that Dragging Canoe had been avoiding her since his return. After the ceremony she approached him.

"So, my cousin, you are now such a great warrior that you do not bother to talk with your little girl cousin, nor do you remember the promises that you have made to her. Was I not promised the first scalp? Where is it? Can I not have it now?"

Dragging Canoe looked away into the distance before he answered.

"Many scalps I could have taken, of course, but I was forbidden by my father to engage in actual combat. Next time, you will see, I will return with many. But I will not let a promise go unrecognized. Meet me by the council house tonight, and I will have something for you."

That night Nanyehi met Dragging Canoe. He presented her with a tiny wooden canoe that looked just like the dugout canoes used by the warriors.

"See? I have carved it myself. It is yours to keep. The first scalp will come later."

Nanyehi was pleased with her present, and she kept it all the years of her life, so that it is even now in the deerskin box with her other sacred things.

There came a time a few years later when Nanyehi was forced to leave her village, and she was not allowed to be with her cousin Dragging Canoe. It was the time when a great sickness came upon the Ani-Yunwiya. It was a sickness with chills and fevers and red bumps and blisters. The Unakas called the sickness "smallpox."

The adawehis tried the usual cure for the sickness with a fever. They treated the sick with fasting, sweat baths, and plunges into the river. But their medicine was not strong enough against this white man's sickness. Many of the Ani-Yunwiya died.

One day when Nanyehi and her mother, Tame Doe, were preparing the evening meal, Attakullakulla entered their cabin.

"The sickness still spreads," Attakullakulla said to his sister. "Today my own son, Dragging Canoe, lies on his mat with the burning fever and chills. Leave the village. Take our mother with you. Travel to the place of spring water on the side of Blue Mountain. At one time our people had a small village there, but now the homes are abandoned and our warriors use them only when they are on the hunt. Stay there for the period of a full moon and then return to the village. Perhaps then the sickness will have been driven from us."

Tame Doe did as her elder brother, the white chief, asked, and she took along with her Nanyehi and Long Fellow, her new son, and Grandmother.

Nanyehi had wanted to go to the house of Dragging Canoe and wish him well, but it was forbidden of her. When the time of the full moon had passed, the small group returned to the village. Immediately Nanyehi asked for her cousin Dragging Canoe.

"Yes, he is well," she was told. "You will find him by the river."

Nanyehi approached the river. She could see the figure of Dragging Canoe. He was bent over as if gazing at something in the water below. At first she thought to creep up behind him and then push him into the river, but something about the position of his body cautioned her not to do this.

Instead she came up quietly and stood behind him until her reflection in the water was visible beside that of Dragging Canoe's. Dragging Canoe looked at her reflection, and she at his. She knew instantly when she saw his face that she must hide her shock, for there in the reflection she could see that the scars of the smallpox had left their mark on Dragging Canoe's face.

"Ha!" she cried to him. And it was then that she gave him a push and sent him toppling into the stream. "I will not be treated so rudely," she called to him as he righted himself and stood up in the water. "I have been gone for a full moon, and when I return you only find time to fish along the banks of the river!"

Dragging Canoe did not join in the merriment as Nanyehi had hoped, however. He shook himself off and then returned to his position along the bank of the river.

Nanyehi sat down beside him and said, "I am glad that you are well. I knew that you would be. You are strong. You will be a great leader for our people as your father is."

"Have you heard?" Dragging Canoe began. "Many did not survive the sickness. Raven, Little Bear, The Mole, and Yellow Corn—they are all gone."

Nanyehi said quietly, "I have heard," and they then sat together silently for a few minutes.

"Do you remember the warrior Crying Wolf?"

"Yes," Nanyehi answered. "Is he not the one who returned from the Creek warpath with four scalps last spring?"

"Yes. He, like myself, survived the sickness. But when he saw his reflection in the looking glass, and realized that the scars left by the healing sores would not go away, he became very angry. He yelled at his wife and treated his mother and friends and relatives with great rudeness, until finally everyone stayed away from him. Then, last week one day, a shot was heard in the direction of the river, and two young boys from the village ran up to say that Crying Wolf's body was floating in the river and that they themselves had seen that he had shot himself."

"Ai-ye! What foolishness!" Nanyehi cried.

"After that, several of the young, unmarried warriors did likewise. Beaver fell on his own spear, and Rock Climber cut his throat with his own knife."

Nanyehi then looked closely into the face of Dragging Canoe.

"You, my cousin, would not do such a thing, would you?"

Dragging Canoe said nothing, but he sat there in silence until Nanyehi became uncomfortable, and she rose and picked up stones and threw them into the river.

Dragging Canoe watched her for a minute, and then he arose and picked up a stone and threw it into the water. And then, with one quick swoop, he picked up Nanyehi and ran into the water and dropped her there so that there was a big splash.

"That will teach you to be so rude to one who will someday be a great chief to his people," he said as he laughed.

So it was that the sickness of the smallpox passed. But it left many behind dead, and many who would carry the scars.

There were those among the Ani-Yunwiya who blamed the Unakas for their tragedy. Dragging Canoe told Nanyehi of this talk. "It is said that the Unakas have brought us this illness. It was brought to us in the whiskey that the Unakas traded for pelts and corn. Everyone knows that it was the warriors who drank the whiskey who first became sick with the smallpox."

But Attakullakulla, his father, was angry when he heard that the people were talking of such things. He called a special council meeting that all of the village might attend.

"Brothers, there has been bad talk these days about our white brothers," he began. "Some would say that they are the ones who have caused the great sickness. Some would even say that they have plotted to kill us by putting the sickness in our whiskey.

"I will tell you that this is not so. For I have been to the white man's camp, and I have seen that they also suffer from the sickness.

"Listen to my words—the white men are our brothers, and the English king, King George, is our great white father. Many years ago, when I was a young brave, I traveled with six of my Ani-Yunwiya brothers across the big water in the canoe of the white man. We were received by our father, the king, and treated by his council with the utmost of favor.

"The king would be our friend and father. He gave us gifts of beautiful clothes and feasted us with his finest food. We, in turn, gave him a crown of possum fur, decorated with scalps and eagle tails.

"We sat in council with our father, King George, and we promised that we would carry the chain of friendship to our people. We told him that we looked upon him as the sun, our father, and that we were his children. We pledged that our hands and hearts would be joined with those of his people. We promised that generation upon generation of our children would be called upon to remember the words said at this council meeting.

"We promised that in war we would be as one with our English brothers, that the great king's enemies would be our enemies, that our people would live and die together.

"We must remember our promises and honor the beloved speech between our people. King George has provided us with guns and ammunition in exchange for friendship and aid. He has sent his warriors to build forts on our land that we may better trade with our white brothers, and that we may protect each other from our enemies, the Creek and the French.

"Let us quit the bad talks about our brothers, the English. Let us remember the chain of friendship between us."

The people listened to the words of Attakullakulla, for he had long held the position of the white chief, the great peace chief of the village of Chota. It was he whose words were heard in the times of peace. It was Oconostota, the red war chief, who was the great ruler in times of war.

Now Attakullakulla was always a friend to the English because he had made the trip to their land across the great water. He kept the paper talks of the speeches of the council meetings with the white brothers with his sacred things. From time to time, he would take out the papers and show them to the traders. Often he would gather the children around and tell them stories of his great trip to the white man's land.

"The white man's canoe," Attakullakulla would tell them, "is larger than our council house. The waves in the water are higher than the trees in our forests. We traveled many days on the water before we came to the white man's land."

Dragging Canoe was impressed by the talk of the white man's weapons.

"They have huge guns," Attakullakulla told the children. "These guns are so large that they must be rolled around on wheels, and they shoot bullets as large as small pumpkins."

Nanyehi loved the stories of the white man's village.

"The king lives in a huge house of stone," Attakullakulla said. "His house is larger than three of our council houses put together. The town where he lives is much larger than Chota. You can walk for a full day and still you will see the houses of the white people. The women ride in small houses that are set on wheels and pulled by horses."

Both Nanyehi and Dragging Canoe realized that the English were a great and powerful people, and they were glad to know that the English were the good friends of the Ani-Yunwiya.

CHAPTER 7
The Ball Play and the Marriage

The paper talks of the white man were passed from Attakullakulla to Beloved Mother when the great chief died. Beloved Mother kept the papers in a box covered with deer hide. There she also kept the wooden canoe from Dragging Canoe and a stone from her mother, Tame Doe, and all of her sacred things.

In the winter evenings, as we sat by the fire, she would take the things from the box and show them to me and tell me their stories. But there was one thing in the box that she never talked of, and for many years I did not ask. It was a scrap of deerskin. One day I became bold and removed this scrap and held it up and asked of her, "Mother, what is this? Why do you keep this old piece of deerskin in the box?"

Mother took the scrap and held it up to the light. It was a small, tattered scrap. The edges were uneven. In some places it was darker, and in some places it was lighter.

"Once it was a larger piece," Beloved Mother said, "but the years have worn it down."

She turned it over several times and then pressed it against her face.

"It was part of the loincloth worn by my first husband, Kingfisher. It was so long ago, and yet when I hold this scrap, it can seem but yesterday. I was only your age when Kingfisher and I were married."

It was on the occasion of the ball play that Nanyehi first observed this young brave, Kingfisher. It was the year when Nanyehi was fourteen.

A messenger from the nearby town of Coyatee arrived at midday. The barking dogs alerted the people that this was no townsman who had come. The villagers paused from their activities as the messenger entered the cabin of Attakullakulla. Many times the messengers brought news of raids by neighboring tribes or of troubles with the Unakas. The people went about their work but glanced back to the chief's cabin from time to time.

When the sun reached the midday sky, Attakullakulla emerged smiling, and the people knew that all was well. He summoned the young brave, Kanati. All watched Kanati intently as he proceeded to the announcement pole. When he reached the top of the pole, Kanati cried out loudly for all to hear, "In fifteen days we people of Chota will meet the people of the Coyatee in the ball play."

Cheers of approval rippled through the crowd, for the ball play was always an occasion of great festivity. The young braves went to their homes and returned with sticks and deerskin balls and were soon at the ball field practicing.

Nanyehi and her two friends, Red Basket and Rising Fawn, decided then that it would be a good time to refill the water jugs, for they would have to pass the ball field on their way to the stream.

Red Basket began talking loudly as they approached the field. She skipped ahead, picking flowers, and shouting to the other two to hurry.

Nanyehi was annoyed. "Do not be so loud. They are only the same boys that we see every day in the village. Why do you put on this strange behavior when we pass them? They will notice you enough if you say and do nothing."

Rising Fawn was watching the players as she passed, and she made the pronouncement, "Dragging Canoe will be the star again. He knows how to take charge and will score more than anyone. Besides, he has the advantage of size; already he is a head taller than our other warriors."

Rising Fawn had been interested in Dragging Canoe for some time. Everyone knew that. They were seen walking together in the evenings at the time of the last Green Corn Festival.

Nanyehi herself had no love interest at that moment. It was true that she thought Kingfisher was attractive. She liked the squareness of his shoulders. Although he was shorter than the other players, he was swift and sure-footed. He would make a good husband, but Red Basket had long had her eye on this young brave. Just last week Nanyehi had observed Red Basket's mother talking with Kingfisher's mother. They were admiring a pair of moccasins and a beaded headband that Red Basket had made. Red Basket would make a very good wife to some young brave.

Still, Nanyehi admired Kingfisher from a distance. Once, she even thought he admired her also, for he had made it a point to come over to speak with her.

It had happened on a late summer afternoon when Nanyehi was watching the small boys of the village playing on the ball field. Her small cousin, Little Bird, was the youngest one, and he could never get the ball. The older ones were too quick and too artful with their sticks. Nanyehi called him to the side and counseled him on this matter.

"You are smaller," she said. "You can get in where they cannot. Do not be afraid to run up to the one with the ball. You will cause him to be off guard. Knock against his stick with your own, and when the ball falls out of the netting at the end, you will catch it. Then you must turn, like this, and you will be off before the larger, clumsier players can catch you."

Nanyehi knocked against the stick of Little Bird, and the ball came flying out of the netted glove. Nanyehi caught it with her own stick and went running down the field

"See? It is easy!" she called back to Little Bird. "Now go and try it yourself."

She watched as he ran to rejoin his teammates, then she turned to walk back to the village; but as she turned, she nearly stepped into Kingfisher, for he was right behind her.

"So," he challenged. "You know the ways of the ball player. I will play you myself in a match."

He handed one of his ball sticks to her. Then he tossed the ball into the air between them.

Kingfisher quickly swooped the ball into the netting of his own stick, out of the reach of Nanyehi.

"Ha!" countered Nanyehi. "If I had not been distracted by the bat I see over there in the tree, I would have had the ball first."

Kingfisher looked toward the tree, for the wings of a bat were always coveted by the ball players, the bat being a creature who can twist and turn and successfully capture any victim. A pair of bat wings on one's stick would assure a player of agility and power in the game. But just as Kingfisher turned to look, Nanyehi knocked her stick sharply against his, and the ball fell out. She quickly scooped it up and ran laughing toward the end of the field as if to score a goal.

When she turned, she saw that Kingfisher had not moved from the spot where he was standing, nor did he make a move to chase after her. Instead he called to her, "So. You win this time." And he turned and headed in the direction of a group of his friends.

After that she saw him several times, but he did not speak to her. She was angry with herself. She had just given him another reason to prefer Red Basket to herself. No young brave wanted to be outdone in a game, especially not by an Indian maiden. Still, as she walked by the ball field each day, she found herself straining to distinguish his form from the other players.

Three days before the ball play she took a blow dart to a nearby grove of trees. She had often seen the bats flying there at the gray time of day, just after the sun had set.

On her third shot, she brought down a bat. She put him into the basket and hurried home. Tame Doe would show her how to re-move the wings and how to preserve them. She thought perhaps to give them to her brother, Long Fellow, or to her cousin Dragging

Canoe. They would bring luck to whomever. She was satisfied with herself that she had thought of a way to contribute to the games. Every member of the village wanted to contribute in some way, for it was believed that the winning of a game would bring health and good luck to the whole village.

On the evening before the game, the townspeople gathered for the customary activities. Nanyehi became anxious, for still she had the bat wings and she did not know to whom she would give them. When she heard the beating of the drums and the rattling of the gourds, she knew that she must hurry to the council square, for the ceremonies were beginning.

As she approached the square, she saw that Oconostota, the red war chief, had taken his place in the center. His face was painted with red and white stripes, the colors of victory and happiness.

Chief Oconostota recited the victories of the Chota team in the games of previous years, then the drummer resumed his drumming and chanting, and the other musicians rattled the gourds. Nanyehi stepped forward in a line with seven girls, each chosen to represent her own clan. They danced forward, extending the heel, then the toe, in time to the beat of the drums.

Then the drumming and the chanting stopped abruptly, and the girls stopped likewise. From the side of the lodge they heard a loud "Haie! Haie!" and Dragging Canoe, the captain of the team, came running out with the other players behind him. They were all painted with red and white stripes. The players circled around the girls and the musicians and echoed a chant with the singing men, "Ehu, Hahi, Ehu, Hahi, Ehu, Hahi!"

Then each player stepped forward, one by one, and pretended to clash with an invisible opponent, knocking him down and stealing the ball.

One of the Chota warriors danced forward, holding the feather of the woodpecker. Now the woodpecker, as all of the Ani-Yunwiya know, has the power to tell the future. The warrior with the feather then shouted, "They are beaten! They are beaten!" The crowd of villagers cheered wildly.

The adawehi arose and announced, "We must now go to water."

Dragging Canoe and the players followed the adawehi to the river for the scratching ceremony. The adawehi scratched each player in turn seven times from his shoulders to his wrist. As the tooth-comb came down, it made seven white stripes which soon turned red. The adawehi also scratched the thighs and legs and finally the chest of each player. The spirits above would be pleased with such a team of warriors, for they had suffered the scratching with no complaint and showed themselves capable of enduring much.

Nanyehi watched the face of Kingfisher, and she was glad to see that he bore the scratching with no sign of pain or fear. When the scratching ceremony had ended, the adawehi called to the crowd, "It is my intent now to inquire into the fate of the ball players of Chota and the ball players of Coyatee."

He held up the black bead as representative of the opposing team, and loudly he called, "Listen, Ha! These people are shaking the road which shall never be joyful for them. The miserable terrapin has come upon them and fastened himself as they go about. They are under the earth. Likewise the blue mole has fastened himself on them. They have lost all strength. The heavy bear has come and fastened himself on them. He has let the stakes slip from their grasp. There shall be nothing left for their share."

The adawehi then held up the red bead, symbolizing the team of their beloved town, Chota.

"But now the players of the town of Chota have risen higher, all the way to the second heaven. The swift flying birds, which by their skill and agility never fail to secure their prey, have come to their aid—the red bat, the great hawk, the martin. The immortal ball stick shall place itself upon the whoop, never to be defeated."

The crowd followed this proclamation with shouts of approval. Oconostota, the war chief, then loudly announced, "We return to the village confident of our victory tomorrow."

Nanyehi stood awkwardly as she watched the players depart. She still had the bat wings. Who should have them? Kingfisher had turned and was walking straight toward the spot where she was standing. She looked at him, and he at her, and neither looked away. But then, just before he reached her, Red Basket came bounding in between them.

"Kingfisher! I have brought you something for good luck. See? It is the feather of a hawk."

"Thank you, Red Basket," Kingfisher said as he took the feather. "I am sure it will bring me the sureness of the hawk. I must go now, though, to be with the other players."

And so he walked on past Red Basket, who stood in confusion, for she had expected Kingfisher to walk her back to the council house, where the people gathered to hear the old stories. Dragging Canoe was walking with Rising Fawn, and Small Otter with Sings-in-the-Wind.

Nanyehi knew that she should turn and begin walking toward the council house herself, but she felt powerless to do so. It was as if she were a tree, rooted to that very spot.

Kingfisher continued to walk forward, and he stopped when he was in front of her. Nanyehi looked down at the ground and then out to the sky. From the corner of her vision, she saw that Red Basket was walking with angry steps back toward the council house. Kingfisher said nothing, so finally Nanyehi spoke.

"I notice you carry three sticks. This is good. If one breaks, then you will have a spare."

"Yes, I have three sticks. It would be good if I had someone to hold this third stick for me while I am in the game, and if one of the others should break, this person could hand me the third."

"I could do that," replied Nanyehi. "I could stand on the side, and if your stick breaks, I would then hand the other one to you, if you would run to the side."

"That would be good," Kingfisher responded, handing her a stick.

"I have these bat wings." Nanyehi ventured. "They will bring the speed and agility of the bat to the ball player who carries them on his stick."

"I could use those bat wings, if I could have someone to help me fasten them to my stick."

"I have these strips of leather with which to fasten. If someone could hold the stick up straight, I could tie on these wings."

"I can do that," said Kingfisher, and they both sat down on the grass to fasten the bat wings. Nanyehi's fingers trembled as she did so. She hoped Kingfisher would not notice, but how could he not? He could probably hear the pounding of her heart. Kingfisher, himself, remained calm and still. When she had finished the tying, he took her trembling hands in his own and said, "Thank you, Nanyehi."

She could not believe that he had said her name. Although she had heard her name said hundreds of times before by others, when he said it, it was as if it had been said for the very first time by the Elder Spirits themselves.

The two of them walked back to the settlement together. The people were gathered around the open square in front of the council house, and Nanyehi and Kingfisher joined them. Already Long Arrow was seated and was beginning to tell the story of the Great Ball Play between the birds and the animals. Long Arrow's voice was low, and all were quiet to better hear the story. He began his story in the usual manner with the words, "This is the story that was told to me by the old men when I was a little boy.

"Once, the animals challenged the birds to a ball play. The birds accepted the challenge, and the leaders of the two groups agreed to a time and place.

"While they were on their way to the playing field, the animals boasted of their strength and skill. The Bear, who was captain of the animals, tossed logs from one side of the road to the other in imitation of how he could throw an enemy player who got in his way. The Terrapin rose up on his hind legs and then crashed his shell to the ground, showing how he could smash an opposing player. The Deer sped along the path, showing how he could outrun any other animal. With his swiftness he would assure his team of the winning goal.

"Now the birds, hearing the boasting of the animals, were somewhat uneasy, although they had a fine team themselves. The Eagle was the captain. The Hawk and the Tlanuwa, who were both strong and swift, were players on the team.

"The birds were roosting in the trees, pruning their feathers and discussing their tactics, when along came two very small creatures climbing up the trunk of the tree. At last these two small things reached the very top of the tree. They crept carefully to the end of the branch and asked Eagle if they might join the game.

"Eagle replied, 'But you are four-legged animals. Why do you not play with the other team?'

"'We have tried,' they answered, 'but we were made fun of for our small size.'

"The Eagle, the Hawk, and the others had a consultation. They felt sorry for these small ones, but how could they join the team of the birds if they had no wings?

"At last one of the birds came up with a solution. They could use the head of the drum to make a pair of wings. They cut two pieces from the head of the drum in the shape of wings, stretched the wings with cane splints, and then fastened them to the front legs of one of the small animals. And thus it was that the birds had now Tlameha, the Bat, to join their team. They threw the ball to him back and forth, and watched with delight as he dodged and circled about, catching the ball with sureness and never dropping it.

"They wanted to fix a pair of wings for the other little creature, too, but there was no leather left. Then someone suggested that they simply stretch his skin. Two of the larger birds took hold of him from opposite sides and stretched the skin between his front and hind legs. And so they created Tewa, the Flying Squirrel. When the ball was thrown to Flying Squirrel, he sprang from a limb after it, caught it between his teeth, and sailed through the air to another branch.

"It was then time for the ball play with the animals. At the first toss of the ball into the air, Flying Squirrel caught the ball and carried it up the tree. Then he threw it to the birds, and they passed it among themselves until it was dropped to the ground. The animals thought it was then their turn to seize the ball, but Bat swooped it up, and he dodged and darted in and out of the other players until finally he himself threw it between the goal sticks, and the birds won the game.

"The Bear and the Terrapin, who had boasted so loudly, never even got a chance to touch the ball."

The people around the fire murmured their approval of the story, for it was a much loved one, and they begged the storyteller to tell another. Kingfisher nudged Nanyehi and said, "I must go now, to spend the night with the other players, for we must all stay in one place the night before the game."

Nanyehi rose early the next morning, as did all the people of the village. Many of them had already gathered near the ball field with blankets and guns and other possessions. There would be much wagering. Even livestock and horses were wagered on this day.

At the designated time, the ball players came from the river, running in a straight line. They had gone this morning for one final cleansing ritual.

Twenty players from each team lined up on the center of the field. The coach from the opposing team threw out the ball, and the ball sticks began to clash as they fought for control of the ball.

Nanyehi was happy to see that Kingfisher, although one of the younger and least experienced players, kept up well with the others. Two men from the Coyatee team scored goals. Then Dragging Canoe and Bluc Dog scored two goals for the Chota team. At one time Kingfisher was in possession of the ball, when in the next minute, Nanyehi could see that there was a crowd of players all on top, and he was under. As the crowd of players peeled off, Kingfisher stood and held up a broken ball stick. Quickly Nanyehi ran down the side of the field and held out the new one.

As she returned to her place, she saw several pairs of eyes upon her. Tame Doe said, "So, I see you are a good friend to Kingfisher now?"

And Nanyehi simply replied, "Yes."

Red Basket was also looking her way, and Nanyehi heard her say to her own mother, "It is true I gave the hawk's feather to Kingfisher, but I gave one also to Blue Dog. I think Kingfisher is too short for me, do you not also?"

The team from Chota won the match, and there was an exchange of many goods. The people were well pleased and looked forward to a year when they would be blessed.

Nanyehi went forward to congratulate Kingfisher, for he also had scored a goal.

Kingfisher, who was usually quiet, was filled with the pride of victory. His voice was excited.

"Did you see?" he asked Nanyehi. "Did you see how I stole the ball from the player with the long legs and how I tripped the shorter one and stole the ball again? Did you see how I whirled the ball between the goal sticks!"

Nanyehi thought at first to tell him how he could have made another goal, if only he had pivoted and charged the player with the long hair instead of running to the outside as he did; but she stopped herself and said instead, "You have done well!"

They made plans to meet after the evening meal, for now Kingfisher would rest and sleep most of the day.

It was on the third day after the ball play that Morning Star, mother of Kingfisher, made a visit to the home of Tame Doe. Both women were dressed in their finest white buckskin. Nanyehi was sent to visit with her friend Laughing Girl while the two women talked.

Three days later, Tame Doe went to the home of Morning Star to discuss Kingfisher's proposal of marriage. Seven days after Tame Doe's visit, Nanyehi was dressed in her white buckskin dress and feasted by the village women in the house of her grandmother. Kingfisher was dressed in his finest buckskin with turkey feathers tied to his hair and was feasted by the men of the village in a lodge close to the council house.

As it came time for the ceremony, the old men entered the council house and seated themselves on the highest seats on one particular side. Next, the old women took the highest seats on the opposite side. Then all the married men entered and took seats by the old men, and then all the married women entered and sat with the old women. The friends of the groom brought him forward to the open space, and the friends of the bride brought her forward also, so that they were standing some distance apart but were facing each other. Kingfisher's mother came forward and gave him a leg of venison and a blanket. Tame Doe then gave to Nanyehi an ear of corn and a blanket.

Nanyehi and Kingfisher then walked forward until they were face to face. They exchanged the words of the wedding vow, then Nanyehi gave Kingfisher the corn, and he gave her the venison. The blankets they joined by folding together to signify to all that they would now live as one.

CHAPTER 8
The Battle of Taliwa

When the messenger from the southern region came, the people expected it would be a message of war. The Creeks and Cherokee had been long-standing border enemies. The enmity went back long ago, to the time when the Creeks had pretended friendship for the Cherokee but had actually come to the aid of the enemy, the Shawano.

The red war chief, Oconostota, called a council meeting. His words were sharp and decisive.

"The crying blood of our ancestors is quenched only with equal blood. The spirits of our departed warriors cannot rest. The friend-knot can never be between our peoples. It is our intent to drive back this enemy forever. We go to war!"

His words found favor with the warriors. Oconostota took up the war drum and marched three times around the council house.

"We leave in three days," he announced.

Nanyehi knew that her husband, Kingfisher, would go to war. It was not required of any brave to do so, but she knew Kingfisher would be among the departing warriors. It mattered not that they now had a small daughter. They had named her Catherine, in honor of a favored trader. Trader Ben had often spoken of his wife in the white settlement of Charles Town. Her name was Catherine.

Kingfisher separated himself from his family immediately on the declaration of war and gathered in the council house with the other warriors. They would engage in three days of fasting and purging, drinking only of the "black drink" prepared by the war women of the tribe in a special ceremony. They would go to water three times a day. They would participate in the scratching ceremony, and only after all this would they be judged worthy of the pursuit of war.

Nanyehi thought to approach Kingfisher.

"I will go, also," she would say. "War women always accompany the men and carry the water and help to prepare the food."

But then she thought better of it, for she knew Kingfisher's answer would be "You must stay here to care for Catherine and the grandmothers. Do not talk of such a thing."

When the time for departure came, she handed Kingfisher a bag of parched corn and a small bundle of supplies.

They then joined the village people gathered at the council square. Guns were fired, and the young warriors whooped and halloed. Chief Oconostota sang the solemn war song and began the war march. The others fell in line, single file behind him, three or four steps from each other. In such fashion they departed the village. The people watched until they were no longer in sight.

When they entered the woods, the war chief signaled a time of silence. They would now proceed with the soft feet of the stalking mountain lion. They would listen with the ears of the wolf and watch with the eyes of the hawk. As the day wore on, they were met by other bands of warriors from nearby Cherokee towns.

It was near nightfall, after the group had made camp, when Nanyehi dared to let her presence be known to Kingfisher. She had stayed all day to the rear of the march with a small group of war women.

"I am here," Nanyehi told him. "Do not waste your strength on anger. I have come to help. Other women have come, too. It has always been this way."

But Kingfisher looked away. How could he not be angry? Why had she said nothing of this to him?

Nanyehi knew his thoughts and responded, "If I had asked, you would have said no. I could not have then broken the beloved speech between us. I had not thought to come, but then last night as I said my prayers before the fire, it seemed that this was to be, and I knew this morning that I must come."

Nanyehi could see that the war raged inside of Kingfisher. She put her hand on his arm, but he turned away from her, squaring his shoulders and lifting his chin. Nanyehi turned to walk away, but before she had taken two steps, she felt Kingfisher's hand as it reached for hers. They walked hand in hand back to the fire of the camp, where they quietly sat and talked.

The next morning they rose early and prepared themselves. Already they were in Creek territory; they would have to be careful. A runner came and announced that the Creeks had learned of their presence and were themselves pressing forward. They were not more than a mile away. Chief Oconostota quickly announced his plan. They would remain in the swamp, where they had the advantage of hiding themselves behind trees and in the bushes. As the enemy advanced, they would take them from their hidden places.

The adawehi was called upon to make his final war proclamation.

"Hayi! Yu! Listen! We have lifted up the red war club of success. We have sent their souls out of motion—to lie under the earth where they shall never reappear. We cause it to be so! There, under the earth, the black foe shall cover them, and they are doomed only to move about there.

"Hayu! Our souls shall be lifted to the seventh heaven. So shall it be! They have been moved on high where they shall forever go about in peace. They are shielded with the white war whoop. They shall never know the blue of failure. It shall be so! Yu!"

Oconostota then addressed his warriors: "I know that your guns are ready! Your tomahawks cry out to the blood of the Creeks; your arrows wait impatiently for their release! Let us not delay. Let us join in force and spirit to forever drive back our enemy, the Creek."

The warriors then positioned themselves and quietly waited. Nanyehi and Kingfisher hid behind a log. Kingfisher's gun was ready. Nanyehi made ready the powder, the packing, and the bullets. She chewed the lead bullets first, for the chewed bullets could better tear apart the victim's skin. They heard the approaching enemy, and suddenly Oconostota let out the distinctive war cry, and everyone sprang into action. Nanyehi was soon in the midst of a raging battle—guns were firing, chewed bullets were flying. The barbed arrows, the javelins, and the tomahawks were now all in motion. Nanyehi kept her back to the log as Kingfisher fired the rifle, and she tried to concentrate on her job.

The Cherokees seemed to be at an advantage. They pushed forward. But then Nanyehi and Kingfisher suddenly found themselves surrounded. A cry to retreat came from Oconostota. Kingfisher eased forward to assess the situation. Things looked clear. He motioned for Nanyehi to follow him. But as he rose again, a zinging bullet ripped through the flesh of his chest, and he fell. Nanyehi was stunned by the suddenness of the action.

"No! It cannot be!" her mind screamed. "Surely the bullet has just grazed his skin. Perhaps he is only stunned!"

But no, she saw the hole in his chest and heard the strange gurgling sounds coming from it. She saw the blood which began to spurt.

Nanyehi looked to the right and left. On either side she could see the Cherokee warriors gathering their things, preparing to retreat. Dragging Canoe, her cousin, motioned to her. A bullet zinged by, and she flattened herself to the ground. She glanced again at Kingfisher. His face was frozen in a rigid grimace, his hand clutched to his chest. She crawled to him and held her ear to his lips, listening for his breath. She heard nothing. Desperately she shook him, but he did not respond.

"Ai-ye!" she cried out. "They cannot have him!"

She was determined to at least save his body from the advancing Creeks. They would not have his scalp.

"Help me! Help me!" she cried to the Spirits above.

She then remembered the story of the Nunnehi and how they had come to the aid of the Cherokee in battles before. Surely they would have pity on her predicament and come to her aid. She sent out a silent prayer to them: "Guide our bullets and our tomahawks! Lead us to victory in this battle!"

Then she stood up and looked to the left and to the right, and she cried out with a loud war whoop. She picked up Kingfisher's rifle and fired. She hit a Creek warrior. He raised his tomahawk, staggered, and fell.

Those around her saw the action and soon rallied to her aid. Word was passed along the line—the tide was turning. They were not to retreat after all, but were to rally and press on. Shouts of encouragement echoed down the lines. The Cherokees pushed back the Creeks and pursued them deep into their own territory. The battle was won!

At sunset the Cherokee warriors gathered their spoils and set up camp. Nanyehi sat for a while with the warriors gathered around the fire, but she became ill at the talk of battle and dying. She withdrew and sat beside the river in the light of the full moon.

Dragging Canoe approached her there.

"My heart grieves for your loss, Nanyehi. We warriors know it was you who won the battle for us. It was your rallying battle cry that sent all into renewed action. Already the word has spread among the hundreds of Cherokee warriors gathered here. Soon the messengers will have spread the news to all of the Cherokee towns. You will be a great and honored woman."

Nanyehi turned to Dragging Canoe. "I do not wish to speak of these things, my cousin. I do not wish to speak to anyone right now. Please ask the others to respect the silence I put between us at this time."

Dragging Canoe looked at her carefully and then said quietly, "I will do this for you."

On the following day they began the march home. That evening, as they gathered by the fire, Nanyehi again sought the solace of the moon and the river. This time her brother, Long Fellow, approached her.

"I have brought you venison stew and corn bread. You must try to eat! You have been through much!"

But Nanyehi refused it and asked her brother to leave her in peace.

On the third night of their return journey, Oconostota approached Nanyehi.

"Nanyehi, I search for the right words, but they do not come. Your grief is mine. Kingfisher was one who knew well the ways of the Ani-Yunwiya. He will be rewarded well by the Elder Spirits above. And you will be forever honored by our people for your contribution at this battle. Both you and Kingfisher are cherished in my heart."

Nanyehi looked at him and said, "Oconostota, I am full of shame. I have betrayed Kingfisher. First, I came without his knowing that I would. Then I witnessed his death in battle. I know him. He would be greatly ashamed that I have witnessed such a thing. Oconostota, I cannot bear that it is in this way that we are to be parted from each other."

Oconostota looked at her gravely. He did not toss her words aside but took them directly to heart. He was quiet for a few minutes, and then he said to her, "Nanyehi, you know, as does Kingfisher, as do all of the Ani-Yunwiya, that it is a great honor to die in battle for one's people. But I do not think these words from me will help you. There is only one who can comfort you, and this one is Kingfisher himself. His spirit still walks close to this earth, for he has not yet been released to the next world. I will leave you here alone. You must talk to Kingfisher. He will release you from your torment."

Oconostota rose and returned to the camp.

Nanyehi sat quietly for a few minutes. She listened as the stream trickled over the rocks. She listened as the leaves of the tree rustled in the breeze overhead. Finally she spoke out softly:

"Kingfisher, I am sorry. I would that we could walk this path of life together for always. You and I—we were as one. My heart grieves for you. Do not be angry with me, Kingfisher."

It was then that she saw the image of Kingfisher, standing above the water. He was dressed in his white buckskin. He spoke to her the words of their marriage ceremony:

"I am never lonely with you."

She responded in like fashion:

"I am never lonely with you."

"The white road of happiness lies before us."

"We will take shelter in the everlasting white house."

"Your soul has come to the very center of my soul, never to turn away."

"My soul lies in the center of your soul, never to turn away."

Nanyehi's spirit went forth to stand next to his. Kingfisher took her hand, and they embraced until they were as one. When they separated, Nanyehi's spirit returned to her body. Kingfisher raised his hand in farewell salute. He then turned and walked upwards, along the white path of happiness, until his form was no longer visible.

CHAPTER 9
Ghigau

After Nanyehi bid her husband farewell, she returned to the camp and lay down. But sleep did not come easily. She heard the call of the coyote and the hooting of the owl. She tossed and turned throughout the night.

True, she had made her peace with Kingfisher, but it was the face of the enemy warrior that now haunted her. She saw again the Creek warrior. He was painted with red vermillion. He wore only his loincloth, as did all the fighting warriors. His hair hung long, down to his shoulders, unlike the short strip of hair on the Ani-Yunwiya warriors. She saw again his face as her own bullet entered his shoulder. He had winced in pain and gritted his teeth. Then he had let out a war whoop and had taken aim with his tomahawk. But before he could release it, he was hit with a second bullet between the eyes. It had been fired by Dragging Canoe, who was close behind Nanyehi. The blood had squirted forward, and his eyes had rolled back. He staggered, then fell.

Perhaps he was the same warrior who had fired the bullet which killed Kingfisher. It could have been him very well, for he was the closest to them, and it was he who was directly in the line of fire.

Nanyehi wondered if his widow knew yet of his death. She wondered if he had any children. She wondered how many warriors had died in this battle.

Nanyehi was startled the next morning when Dragging Canoe shook her gently, and she saw that the sun was out and that all were readying to leave.

"It is time, Cousin. We travel all day and tomorrow also. We must go."

Nanyehi blinked back from the sunlight. She looked about. The world was the same. The trees still stood, and the squirrels chattered from them. The sun was beginning its daily climb in the sky. The wind blew gently. Somehow she could not believe that all would be the same. How indifferent the world was to the pain and destruction that had just occurred!

As the warriors traveled, they laughed and joked among themselves. She wondered how it was that they could carry on so. How was it that her own body could continue to function so easily? For she found that she could still walk, and she could still swing her arms, and already she felt hunger pangs and ate of the food when the time for meals came.

In the late afternoon of the third day they reached their beloved town of Chota. Oconostota sent a runner ahead with the war stick. It would be placed at the council house, signifying to the people that they had been victorious. It was decorated with seven scalps painted on the underside with red vermillion.

Meanwhile the warriors set up camp at the river, some distance away from the town. The blood of battle was still upon them. They must observe the proper cleansing ritual before they could be reunited with the villagers.

The adawehi led the warriors into the river—one by one, they waded out, and he dipped with the sacred gourd and poured the cleansing water over them.

Then he lifted his voice loudly, "Yu! We have lifted our red war clubs! We have sent the enemy to the spirit world. They are bound by a black net to the world below.

"Long Man River now lets his water flow over you, cleansing you of the blood of the enemy. You are now clothed in white. You are to tread the white road, and you will now dwell in the house of white. This shall be so! You are now released!"

The warriors then returned to the village, but Nanyehi remained behind at the water's edge. Dragging Canoe returned to talk with her. He knelt beside her.

"They call your name, Nanyehi. The people of Chota call your name. The messengers say every town in the world of the Ani-Yunwiya has heard of your feat. They say it is you who claim the victory, for we were in the process of retreat when your battle cry was heard and passed on. Come back to the village with me."

Nanyehi said nothing; she sat motionless, her faced bowed.

Dragging Canoe continued. "The people say Nanyehi truly walks with the Spirit People. Her medicine is strong."

Nanyehi looked out to the water, then spoke:

"Tell them I mean no disrespect, but I am in mourning. Grief is heavy upon me. Ask that they respect the quiet way of the grieving widow and not disturb her peace. I will camp here another day. I am not yet ready to go back."

Dragging Canoe said nothing then, but he placed his hand lightly on her shoulder to show his agreement. Then he rose and returned to the village.

It was Tame Doe, mother of Nanyehi, who then made her way to the riverbank. She brought the child, Catherine, with her.

"Welcome, my daughter," Tame Doe said as she embraced Nanyehi. Catherine squealed and lunged forward with arms outstretched to her mother.

Nanyehi's eyes filled with tears. This one looked so like her father.

"Ai-ye!" she said to her. "Who is this little one? Has she been a good girl for her grandmother? How pretty and chubby she looks!"

Tame Doe spoke. "Come now, Nanyehi. Return with us to the village."

But Nanyehi handed her daughter back to her mother and looked away. "I will stay here for a while longer. I cannot go back now."

"I think it best not to leave you alone at this time, Nanyehi," Tame Doe protested.

"It will be as I say, Mother." Nanyehi knew her words were sharp.

She hoped they did not sting, but she knew she must remain here. She was not ready to go back.

Tame Doe turned and made her way up the path to the village.

It was Grandmother who next came. She said nothing at first, but simply sat beside Nanyehi in silence.

Finally she handed Nanyehi a corn cake and said, "Let us heat a little water, and I will fix some tea."

Nanyehi ate the corn cake and watched as Grandmother built the fire and prepared the water. When the vapors began to rise from the water, Grandmother threw in the gooseberry leaves, and they watched as the water darkened. Grandmother then dipped a cup for herself and one for Nanyehi.

When they finished the tea, Nanyehi spoke. "I am still unclean, Grandmother. I partook of the cleansing ceremony as did the others, but still I feel unclean. The blood of the dead rests upon me."

"Nanyehi, it was I who brought you to the water on your first day of life. You and I, let us go to water again now, as we did on that first day."

Grandmother removed her moccasins and waded out. Nanyehi followed her.

Scooping the water into her hand, Grandmother poured it over her own head and then over Nanyehi. Nanyehi then also scooped the water and poured it over her head.

When she opened her eyes, she looked at Grandmother. Grandmother's gaze was fixed on the bank of the opposite shore. Nanyehi's eyes followed hers. There, standing near the water's edge, was a white wolf. He let out a low howl in greeting to them.

Grandmother said softly, "Hail, Brother Wolf. This one has done well."

Then there was above the white wolf a group of warriors, talking among themselves. Nanyehi could see that it was Kingfisher and Crying Man and Corn Eater and other warriors who had been killed in the recent battle. But they did not see Nanyehi or Grandmother or anything else around them. Instead they talked among themselves and then turned and walked straight along the white road to the upper world above.

The wolf then rose and turned and headed into the woods.

Nanyehi looked at Grandmother. "Did you see it, also?"

Grandmother nodded. The two of them waded back through the river and sat down again upon the bank.

"Nanyehi," Grandmother began, "I have never told you this. I have never told anyone. The white wolf was here on the first day of your life. He was here at this river as he was here today. Our brother, the wolf, is a messenger from the spirit world; we must think carefully on his message."

Nanyehi said, "It is time I now returned."

As Nanyehi and Grandmother made their way to the cabin, the people stopped their tasks and nodded as they passed. Nanyehi simply nodded in return; she did not talk. They likewise respected her silence and did not address her. But she heard their comments to each other as she passed. "It is she—Nanyehi. It is said she walks with the Spirit People."

Nanyehi feared to enter her cabin, for this was the place where she and Kingfisher had built their first fire together and lived and dwelled as man and wife. When she entered the cabin, she looked about. Kingfisher's things were no longer on the wall—his ball sticks, his moccasins, his sleeping mat. All had been removed.

Tame Doe spoke. "I have gathered all of Kingfisher's things for you. Some of them you will want to keep, no doubt. Some you may want to give to his family."

A voice, calling from the door, diverted their attention. Tame Doe went to the door and stepped outside. Nanyehi could hear the conversation.

"We bring these otter skins for Nanyehi. She has no warrior now to provide for her. She has fought so bravely for all of us. We are deeply grateful."

"Thank you, Star Woman," Tame Doe replied. "I will see that she gets them. She will be pleased. Now she is resting."

Tame Doe brought the otter skins inside. But no sooner had she turned around than there was another voice at the door.

This time time it was Kanati with a deer pelt, and behind him was Lame Elk with a wampum belt and then Crying Woman with a rabbit pelt. As Tame Doe looked out, she saw that the people of the village had made a line all the way back to the council square, and all were standing with pelts and wares.

Tame Doe turned to Nanyehi. "Daughter, I think it would be better if you would come out."

Nanyehi looked out upon the people. She stepped outside and raised her hand in greeting to those gathered. Black Hawk came forward and handed her the deerskin. Nanyehi said, "Thank you, Black Hawk." One by one, she accepted the gifts brought by the villagers, giving a word of recognition and thanks to each person.

That evening, Nanyehi retired and slept the whole night through without awakening.

The next few days were spent by the people in feasting and celebration. The third day was the appointed day for the ceremonial recognition of the warriors. The people gathered in the council house. The drums were beating. The returned warriors were dressed in ceremonial clothes—red-dyed moccasins and leggings of otter skin. Their skin glistened with bear oil. Nanyehi was dressed in her white buckskin dress.

Oconostota, the red war chief, and Attakullakulla, the white peace chief, stood on a small platform.

Oconostota began the ceremony. He was in the ceremonial dress of the warrior chief. The raven head draped across his breast, and the wings draped over his shoulder. Eagle feathers were tied to his scalp.

"My people, we have returned from the land of the Creek victorious. We observed strictly the laws of purity—we fasted for three days, we went to water, we partook of the black drink. The Divine

Spirits saw our good efforts, and we were rewarded.

"I will tell you of the conduct of our warriors. We did not behave as the blind white man who rushes into battle with eyes shut. No! As we entered the enemy territory we crept from tree to tree, from rock to rock, from log to log. Our braves crawled through the swamps. They covered their footsteps with bear paws. They walked along the stream where footsteps could not be found. The Creeks could not discern our movements, and it was thus that we overtook them.

"Let us now honor those warriors who have distinguished themselves in battle. May you who stand before us watching today, you who would be warriors in the future, be heartened by the honors you see being given today."

As Oconostota spoke, the white chief, Attakullakulla, stepped forward. He had at his side a collection of crowns of swan feathers.

Oconostota called forward the first warrior. "Young Deer, formerly a gun carrier, has taken a scalp and has acquired the rank of 'Man Killer.'"

Chief Attakullakulla placed a crown of swan feathers on his head.

The young brave whooped with joy and circled the council house three times and then resumed his place. Blue Dog and Otter and many others were also honored with the title of "Man Killer." Dragging Canoe, who boasted the most scalps taken, was given the title of "Great Warrior." He was presented with the much coveted eagle feather. When all the warriors had been thus recognized, Oconostota spoke again.

"We have one among us who has earned the title of special distinction. It is equal in rank to 'Greatly Honored Man.'

"This one lost her beloved warrior in battle. But she did not take pity on herself or throw herself to the enemy in panic, but rather she took up the gun of her fallen husband and cried the war cry. And thus it was that we were spared the agony of defeat, and celebrate instead the dance of victory. Nanyehi will be known henceforth as 'Ghigau,' Beloved Woman. In such a position she will be a member of the War Council and will be head of the Women's Council."

Nanyehi stepped forward, and her uncle Attakullakulla presented her with the cape of swan wings, which would remain her emblem of distinction.

When Nanyehi resumed her position in the line, Oconostota spoke to the newly honored group: "Remember what you are this day according to the old beloved speech."

Before the people dispersed, however, there was another matter to be decided. When all had quieted, Oconostota spoke again:

"We have taken from the Creeks one black slave which we now present to Ghigau, Beloved Woman, in honor of her great deed. We have taken other captives who were Creek warriors. We leave the fate of these captives in the hands of the Women's Council, as is our custom. Our women will now meet here in the council house to determine the fate of those taken."

The warriors and the men then departed, and the women gathered in the semicircle of council seats. Nanyehi awkwardly took the head position. She looked about at the faces of the women gathered around her. How could she occupy such a position of authority when she was only eighteen years of age?

It was Grandmother who then spoke. "Ghigau, we are ready to begin the discussion. We wait for your approval."

Nanyehi took a deep breath and responded. "Let us consider the fate of our captives. Shall they be put to death, or shall they be adopted into our tribe?"

Red Basket spoke first. "We should torture them and burn them at the stake! We must obey the law of vengeance. These captives shall be killed to avenge the spirits of our own departed warriors. My own brother was among them, and I wish to know with assurance that he is on his way to the other worlds. The law of vengeance says our departed cannot be released to the heavens above until their deaths have been avenged."

Yellow Bird agreed. "Yes. We shall tie them to the stake, then they will be tortured and burned. I have lost my husband. His spirit demands our vengeance."

Others agreed with these first two speakers. Nanyehi allowed all who desired to speak a turn. Then she rose and quietly said, "I, too, have lost my husband. I, too, am concerned that our warriors be allowed to enter into the next world. I must tell you of the vision that I had upon my return to Chota. Grandmother was there, too, and she will verify the truth of my story."

Nanyehi paused and looked out gravely to those seated before her. Then she continued. "It happened at the river. Grandmother and I walked into the water to cleanse ourselves. We saw a wolf on the opposite bank, a white wolf."

The women gasped as she said this. Basket Weaver, an old and respected woman, spoke. "The white wolf is our blood brother. He brings us a message from the spirit world."

"What does it mean?" the women asked of her.

Basket Weaver replied, "White is the color of peace and happiness."

Nanyehi spoke again. "I believe it means that I am to be the voice of peace for our people. Often the woman who goes to war and distinguishes herself is considered a war woman. But it will not be so with me. I will be the voice of peace and will lead as the great peace chief does."

Nanyehi looked about and saw others nod their heads in agreement.

"I will tell you the rest of my vision," she continued. "Behind the white wolf there appeared our beloved husbands, sons, and brothers who were killed in battle. Kingfisher was there, as was Crying Man and Corn Eater and all the others. They talked among themselves, but they did not see us. They turned from us and walked the white path to the spirit world above."

The women whispered among themselves. "What does she say?

What is meant by this?"

It was then that Grandmother spoke to the group. "I have thought on this vision, and the meaning of the message brought by the white wolf is now clear to me. Our beloved husbands and brothers have traveled the road to the higher places. They have been released. There is no need for further vengeance or shedding of blood. We have already killed many of them. Let us, then, adopt these captives into our tribe."

The women murmured among themselves. Many agreed with Grandmother, but others spoke of their fears. "This is not good. What of our men taken in battle? Do you think the Creeks would be so good to them?"

Nanyehi was quick with an answer.

"We will release one prisoner. He will make his way back to the tribe. He will tell the Creeks that none of their people were tortured in captivity. He will tell them we adopted the prisoners into our tribe and that the Great Spirit spoke to us through the white wolf, and so it is to be."

Nanyehi looked at the women. Raven Woman and Burning Tree and New Moon nodded in approval. Red Basket and Yellow Bird sat with tight faces. Nanyehi knew they would have liked to have tortured the prisoners. It was a spectacle they enjoyed. But they said nothing, and so their silence was accepted as agreement.

"It is decided then," she said. "Let us now look to our captives. Those of you who have lost a son or husband will be the ones to choose."

Thus it was that Nanyehi became Beloved Woman of the town of Chota in the days when the Ani-Yunwiya were a great and mighty people. And thus it was that she first presided over the Women's Council.

But there were those who were not happy with the decision of the Women's Council. The next day Dragging Canoe approached Nanyehi. "This is not good, Cousin. We should not let all the captives live. The Creeks will hear of this, and they will be much bolder in battle and more quick to go to war. For what should they now fear? To be captured would not be such a dreadful event."

Nanyehi looked carefully at Dragging Canoe. She knew that she looked at one who would one day be a great chief to her people. Everything about Dragging Canoe attested to this—his physical strength, his courage in battle, his ability to inspire the other men to action.

"Cousin," she replied, "the Great Spirit has spoken to me through the white wolf. This is the way it is to be."

Dragging Canoe looked at her for a moment, then turned and walked away. Nanyehi knew then that her cousin's path would be a different path—he would be a great chief and warrior, and he would follow the red road of war.

CHAPTER 10
How Nanyehi Came to Marry Bryant Ward

One of the scrolls in the box of sacred things is tied with red ribbon. It is the official marriage decree of Beloved Mother and her second husband, Bryant Ward. Beloved Mother has always said that it is the words on paper that the white man considers to be the sacred word.

So it was that when Beloved Mother was married to the white trader, Bryant Ward, the official paper was made. I, myself, can now read these words: "On the 18th day of September, 1756, Bryant Ward, a subject of the British crown, and Nanyehi of the Cherokee nation were joined in the bond of holy matrimony. By the power of the King of England and the Holy Church, they shall be declared as one."

For the people of the Ani-Yunwiya, the Principal People, the word spoken at the council fire with the smoking of the peace pipe, that is the sacred word. It is believed that the smoke of the peace pipe carries the message of the beloved words to the spirit world above, and thus the words are sacred and will be honored by all above and below.

The paper words of the Unakas have been a mystery to our people, for they have no way of reaching the Spirit Beings above. Perhaps that is why the white people do not honor their agreements.

I myself have never trusted the Unakas. I am afraid of them. I know it has to do with the memories of the first part of my life. But Beloved Mother has always been the friend of the white settler. Her daughters, Catherine and Elizabeth, have married white men and live in the white settlements. I do not go with her to visit these families, for I am still not comfortable with the white people.

Beloved Mother grew up with the Unaka traders. It was through Attakullakulla that she learned respect for them, for Attakullakulla was always a friend of the white trader.

In the early days there were different kinds of Unakas. There were the English, the sons of King George. To them we signed allegiance when Attakullakulla and the other warriors traveled to their land. There were the French, who also wished to be our friends and who fought against the English for control of the land. Then there were the settlers who came from England but who later wanted to break their allegiance to that country and form a new, independent country.

It was Attakullakulla who constantly cited our friendship with the British. It was he who helped to establish the building of Fort Loudoun, which brought more English traders into the area and which was kept stocked with soldiers who would protect the land for the Ani-Yunwiya and the English.

It was Attakullakulla who first suggested to Nanyehi that she marry Bryant Ward.

Those were the days when the ways of the Ani-Yunwiya were changing. The women clamored for the iron pots and the calico cloth and the spinning machines. The Ani-Yunwiya warriors wanted iron tools, guns, and ammunition. The men began hunting not just to provide food for their families, but also to provide skins to trade.

The Ani-Yunwiya needed the goods of the white man, and the white man needed the friendship of the Indians to trade and settle on the land. The leaders of both groups looked for ways to strengthen ties. The white traders who lived in the Ani-Yunwiya villages helped to do this, but they could only live in the villages if they took a Cherokee wife.

So it was that Attakullakulla made a special visit to the home of Nanyehi. He waited, however, until he saw Tame Doe depart with a basket for gathering herbs. Then he quietly entered the cabin and approached his niece.

"He is a good man, Nanyehi," Attakullakulla said of Bryant Ward. "I know him, and he wants you. He has requested that I speak with you. He would be a good husband."

"But I am in mourning," Nanyehi protested. Her widened eyes told Attakullakulla she had not yet heard the talk in the village about this matter. "And I have this new one here to take up all my time," she added as she gestured to the small sleeping form on the bearskin.

The new baby, Short Fellow, son of Kingfisher, was born six months after the death of his father and was now only three months old.

Attakullakulla spoke again. "It has been nearly a year since the death of Kingfisher. The Ani-Yunwiya have never required a long mourning period. I, as head of your family, declare that you are no longer in mourning."

"What is this, Father?" A voice from the doorway soon alerted Attakullakulla that this matter would not be so easily decided. Dragging Canoe stooped so that his tall frame might enter. "I have heard that you come to Nanyehi to propose her marriage to Ward, the Englishman."

"It would be a good marriage for all," Attakullakulla explained. "For our people, for the English, for Nanyehi, for Bryant."

"This will not be good. Soon Nanyehi will be living in the white world," Dragging Canoe protested.

"No. Bryant will be accepted into our world. He will live with us in the village, as do the other traders. Their children will be of the wolf clan, and they will be raised as members of our tribe."

"That is what our laws say," countered Dragging Canoe, "but you can see for yourself—Smiling Face and Yellow Leaf—they now live outside of the village and wear the dresses of the Unakas. Their children go to the white schools."

There was then another voice from one who had just entered the room.

"What?" Tame Doe demanded. "I am the mother of this one, and I will make the arrangements if there is to be a marriage. Why am I not being consulted? Attakullakulla, I cannot believe you would be so disrespectful!"

"I only came to tell her she is no longer in mourning, Sister." Attakullakulla lamely defended himself.

Nanyehi looked at all three of them.

"It is I who will make the decision," she said loudly and clearly. Then she turned to Attakullakulla, "I had thought to remarry, Uncle. But I thought to marry a warrior of our tribe and bear more children for our people."

Attakullakulla looked away. He paced to the door and then turned and came back again.

"I knew these would be your thoughts, Nanyehi, but I have talked to the warriors. All agree that you are the most beautiful woman of our tribe and that it would be a great honor to be your husband. But that is part of the problem. You have led men in battle; you have been spoken to by the Spirit People; you hold the position of Beloved Woman of our tribe. There is no one in our ranks now who feels he could be equal to you. I have given it much thought, Nanyehi. It is so!"

Nanyehi opened her mouth to protest, but instead she stopped and looked at her cousin Dragging Canoe. He was silent. His arms were crossed in front of him. His eyes were on his feet below.

"Dragging Canoe, do you agree?" Nanyehi asked.

Without looking up, Dragging Canoe nodded his assent.

All were quiet until Nanyehi herself spoke. She took a deep breath and said, "Tell Mr. Bryant Ward to come for the evening meal tomorrow. The squirrels are thick now. Tomi will shoot some, and Mother and I will prepare a meal."

Attakullakulla's face lighted, and he nodded happily in agreement.

Tame Doe called out to him as he left, "Tell Mr. Ward to bring two iron pots and a parcel of blue cloth as proof of his good intentions."

Nanyehi then turned to Dragging Canoe. He was looking at her. His eyes were not hard, but soft. His words were serious, but they were not sharp.

"I will watch this Unaka, Nanyehi. If he is not worthy of you, I will see that he leaves. And if he is a good man, I will say no more. But remember, Nanyehi, you and I, we are Ani-Yunwiya. I hope to be a great chief, and you are the Beloved Woman of Chota. Do not leave our people, Nanyehi."

Nanyehi's words were scolding. "Your words, my cousin, are insulting. How could I ever leave my people? They are always foremost in my mind. It is an insult to be thus reminded. Do I remind you of your loyalties?"

Dragging Canoe then smiled. He had grown up with this one, but he was still surprised at Nanyehi's strength sometimes. Nanyehi smiled likewise, and Dragging Canoe departed.

On the next evening Bryant Ward was there with a parcel of blue cloth and two iron pots. He had a doll for Catherine and a bow and arrow for Short Fellow, who was, of course, too young to know of such things.

"I have brought someone else," he added. "Please come outside and see."

Tame Doe and Nanyehi followed him outside. Standing by the front porch was a young black woman. She had short hair, and she was dressed in a cloth of blue that wrapped around and tied above one shoulder.

"I bought her in Charles Town," Bryant said. "She is called Oni. She will make a good wife for your black slave, Tomi."

Nanyehi glanced at Tomi. He pretended to be busy with his task of bringing in the firewood.

"What do you think, Tomi? Would this suit you?" Nanyehi asked.

Tomi then looked up, and a smile spread across his face. "This would be well with me, Ghigau," he said.

"So will it be then," replied Nanyehi. "You will show her around today, and tomorrow she will work with Mother and me."

Tame Doe's face was beaming. No doubt, she thought, this generous man would make a good son-in-law.

Nanyehi said simply, "I thank you." She was touched by the gesture, but she would reserve her judgment for now.

After dinner Bryant suggested they walk on the path by the river. Tame Doe urged her on.

"I will mind these two," she said of Catherine and Short Fellow.

And so it was for five nights. Bryant Ward came for supper, and they walked and talked afterward on the path by the river. On the fifth night Bryant declared his intention.

"I ask that you marry me, Nanyehi. I have wanted you for a long time."

Nanyehi looked at him questioningly. "A long time?"

"I was there at the Battle of Taliwa when you led your people. I watched the whole battle from the overlooking hillside. I saw your people rally to your cry. You cannot be more than eighteen years of age, but already your people know and respect you. I have heard that it is by your words that the Creek captives were not tortured and killed. You are the most beautiful and the most desirable woman I have ever met. I want you to be my wife."

Nanyehi searched his eyes. His words came as a surprise. He had said that he had wanted her for a long time. She had thought he wanted her because it was a good business move. Many of the white traders took Indian wives so that they could live protected in the Cherokee towns. But now he was telling her that it was she herself that he wanted.

She was silent for a few minutes as she thought on these things. She was moved by his words. Had he not brought her fine gifts? Had not her uncle attested to his good character? And though she knew Uncle Attakullakulla could take advantage of a situation, she knew him to be honest in all his undertakings.

Still, this was not a step to be taken lightly, and there were things about it that must be considered.

"You have no white wife?" she asked.

"My wife died three years ago in her home country of Ireland. I have a son there who is being raised by my wife's sister."

"You would live with me in my village?"

Bryant nodded.

"Our children would be Ani-Yunwiya?"

Again he nodded.

"And you would observe the practice of our people that says that the Ani-Yunwiya goes to water every morning unless he is sick or otherwise unable?"

At this last question, Bryant's eyebrows went up and his jaw dropped.

Nanyehi continued, "It's just that we are a people who go to water often. I do not see how you Unakas cannot do so. Do you not know that unless you go to water you have a strong smell?"

At this Bryant laughed. "For you, I will go to water."

Then he coughed. "But often times I have a cough." He coughed loudly this time and pounded his chest. "It may be necessary to bring the water to me."

It was Tame Doe who insisted that they go to Fort Loudoun for the official ceremony. Privately she told Nanyehi: "This will not be the marriage that some of the traders have. They have a white wife in the white man's town and an Indian wife in the Indian village. You will have the white man's ceremony, and you will have the white man's paper to prove it to the white man's world."

Nanyehi could see no harm in this idea. Besides, she welcomed the chance to see the town of the white man; and she suspected that this was true of Tame Doe also, for Tame Doe insisted that she must go as a proper escort.

Thus it came to be that Beloved Mother's marriage was recorded on the sacred scroll, which even now remains in the deerskin box with the other sacred things.

CHAPTER 11
How the War with the Unakas Began

In the first year of their marriage, things went well with Bryant and Nanyehi. Their daughter, Elizabeth, was born. Their home was extended so that now there was a room for cooking, a room for sleeping children, a room for sleeping adults, and a room for receiving guests. Many guests came to visit—both the white traders and the men and women of Chota. It was the white traders who addressed Beloved Mother as Nancy, for they found it easier to pronounce than Nanyehi. Thus she came to be known as Nancy Ward to the government officials and the people of the white settlements.

Oni and Tomi, the black slaves, also had a cabin and began a family of their own. They helped with the crops, for Bryant and Nanyehi had a large garden where they grew potatoes, beans, peas, squash, and pumpkins.

Bryant bought seven horses, which he used as pack animals and for riding. Also, he purchased a small herd of pigs. The white man liked the meat of the pig, and it was easy to preserve.

Of course Dragging Canoe made an official protest. He said to Nanyehi, "Ha! Now you raise pigs! It is as I said! I hope you do not eat of these animals yourself or you will move slowly and lazily as the pig lover does."

"The pig we raise, so that we may trade the meat to the whites for other things such as the gun and ammunition you carry, Dragging Canoe," Nanyehi retorted.

Bryant Ward traveled to Fort Loudoun for trade with the English. Sometimes he took Nanyehi with him. But there came a day when it was no longer safe for Bryant to travel to the fort.

Now it was in those days that the British fought against the

French. The Cherokee warriors were happy to help their brothers, the English. But all did not always go so well. There were many misunderstandings which resulted in bloodshed for both the white man and the red man. Oconostota, the red war chief, called a council meeting that these matters might be discussed.

Nanyehi, as Beloved Woman, sat near the fire in the center of the council house. Beside her were the head men of Chota and also the chief men from neighboring villages. She looked about at the people gathered before them. Her vision was dimmed by the darkness of the council house and by the smoke from the center fire. But she could make out the forms around her, and she saw that the benches, rising in circles from the center, were all filled with warriors and women, and that others were left standing in the doorway and out in the council square. Many people had come to hear these talks. They sat in a hushed manner to better hear the words of the chief men.

Oconostota opened the talks. "We all know of the bad happenings in these last years. Moytoy will tell of his grievances."

Moytoy, the great war chief of Settico, then spoke. "My warriors fought bravely for our English brothers in the battle against the French. We lost twenty of our horses in battle. The English warriors at the fort would not replace them. We were told to find our own horses.

"We took then twenty horses we found on the open range, only then to be told that they belonged to the white settlers and we must return them. This we refused to do, for it was our right to have twenty horses!

"The Unaka soldiers attacked us and killed nineteen of our warriors. We avenged the death of our warriors and killed nineteen Unaka settlers. It was then that the Virginia government laid a bounty on our scalps, and we lost forty more warriors!"

Nanyehi watched the reaction of the chiefs gathered. The older chiefs took all this in and sat quietly for a time. But the younger chiefs were agitated and talked among themselves with angry looks and threatening gestures.

Dragging Canoe then rose and spoke: "My father is a good friend to the English, and he would not speak against them, but I will tell you of the humiliation he has endured. It was Attakullakulla who rode out to discuss the matter of Moytoy's warriors in hopes to come to a peaceful settlement. When he arrived in Virginia, he was told by the Unaka warriors that he and his band would have to serve as scouts at that very time."

The murmurs of disapproval could be heard in the council house.

"When Father protested that he had come in the rank of chief warrior and was there only to discuss the peace settlement, the soldiers put him and the warriors with him in their jail. He was finally released by order of the government, and he is now on his way to speak on these matters with Governor Lyttleton in Charles Town. I advised him not to go, because who can tell in what manner he will be received."

Dragging Canoe allowed the message of his words to rest in the minds of the chiefs gathered. He then told them of the words sent by messenger:

"Tomorrow one of the Creek chiefs, The Great Mortar, arrives. He would speak with our chiefs, for the Creeks are much grieved also by the actions of the white man."

Voices of surprise could be heard throughout the council house. For a chief of the Creek nation to address a Cherokee council meeting, the matter must be one of grave importance. Nanyehi waited until the rumblings had ceased. She then stood and looked out to her people. She spoke loudly and distinctly.

"Brothers, Attakullakulla is not here with us, but I would speak for him and share with you the words in his heart. The happenings that we discuss were all misunderstandings. We are two separate peoples, the white men and the red men. Our ways are different. We must come to know each other's ways that we may avoid further bloodshed.

"It is true the Creek chief arrives tomorrow. But since when are the Creeks our friends? They have proven to be our enemy since the days of the Shawano War, when they pretended to be our trusted friends and instead went to the aid of the Shawano. You would trust their friendship on these matters then today?

"Are we to abandon now our allegiance to the British, who have promised to be our protectors and with whom we have signed the sacred agreements? The white chiefs assure us that these matters will be dealt with, and thus Attakullakulla journeys now to talk with them. Let us then continue to cultivate our friendship, and may no more blood be shed."

Nanyehi looked upon the faces of the chiefs gathered. She could see that many were in agreement, but others sat rigidly with arms crossed and squared jaws.

On the following day, The Great Mortar, chief of the Creeks, arrived and sat in council with the Ani-Yunwiya chiefs. Oconostota took the tobacco from his pouch and lit his pipe and then passed it to The Mortar. The Creek chief first held up the pipe in admiration, for it was a beautiful pipe. The rounded bowl was cut from red stone, and the long stem was decorated with porcupine quills and dyed feathers. The Mortar put the pipe to his lips, drew from it, and passed it on to the other chiefs gathered. He then made his speech:

"Brothers, your sisters and your mothers mourn their departed warriors killed by the British. We know that the British have no respect for the ways of the red man. They do not respect our property; they do not respect the agreement of the peace pipe ceremonies. It is only recently that two British warriors, drunk on whiskey, entered the home of one of our families and raped two of our wives while their husbands were on the hunt."

Again the murmurs of anger and disapproval rumbled through the council house. The Great Mortar waited until all had quieted. Then he continued:

"Let us then take up the hatchet for the King of France, who will treat us as equals and who will furnish us with supplies!"

Now most of the chiefs shared the opinion of Nanyehi and Attakullakulla and did not trust the Creeks. But there were those among the group who would take up with the Creek. These were Saloue, chief of Estatoe, and Wauhatchie, chief of three lower Cherokee settlements. It was these chiefs who then rode with the Creek warriors and raided the settlements of the Carolina frontier. Soon the war dance spread to other lower Cherokee settlements, and they also participated in the raids.

Attakullakulla, when he returned, was greatly distressed at this news and also at the word brought by his messengers.

He spoke to Nanyehi and Dragging Canoe. "These happenings are not good. It is said the Governor has fifteen hundred men ready to march against our towns. He will not be satisfied until our people have been taught a lesson! Oconostota will ride out for the peace talks this time. He and I have discussed these matters. We have agreed on a list of twenty-eight chiefs who will travel with him. Surely the white governor will see our serious intention of peace."

"No, Father! Our chiefs will not be safe!" protested Dragging Canoe.

"The Governor has guaranteed their safe passage. You and I will remain behind and await the news," Attakullakulla answered.

It was the cold, white of wintertime when the chiefs left, but it was not until the thawing time of spring when they returned. Messengers had gone back and forth, and Nanyehi and the others of Chota knew that all did not go well. But no one was prepared for the news that Oconostota brought when he finally retuned.

"My brothers and sisters," began Oconostota, "we must prepare ourselves. There have been terrible things that have happened. We were not received by our white brothers in the manner that was promised us by the Governor. We were confined to a guarded cabin, too small even for five people. In this we were all forced to stay.

We were guarded as prisoners. After much talk I was allowed to leave, but the others were not.

"The Unakas repeatedly ignored my demand for the release of our chiefs. I determined that action must be taken. My men killed one British chief and injured two of his warriors. In return, our chiefs were killed—all twenty-eight of them!"

Nanyehi heard then the cries of mourning of her people. She knew that this great loss would soon be avenged by the Ani-Yun-wiya warriors.

Oconostota continued his speech. "We cannot live in peace with the white soldiers any longer. The blood of our departed chiefs and warriors cries out to us. We are a strong and powerful nation. It is time we drive this intruder from our land!"

So it was that on the next morning the chiefs and warriors made their plans. It was agreed that Willenawah and Standing Turkey would lead the warriors in a siege of Fort Loudoun.

"We will surround the fort and not allow any supplies to pass in," said Oconostota. "We will force the Unakas to surrender, and then we will evict them from our land!"

When Nanyehi heard these words, she knew the times were not good for any white man in the Cherokee land. She rushed from the council meeting to speak with her husband, Bryant.

"You must leave! Now!" she told him.

"But these are your people. They have accepted me as one of them. I will be safe here. They will not harm me."

"They do not all know you! They do not all like you! They do not all agree that a white man should be in our settlement. Twenty-eight of our chiefs have died. Our warriors will not rest until twenty-eight Unakas have died, and some of them will not care much which Unaka it is! I tell you, you are in great danger! You must leave!"

"But what of Betsy and you and the other children? I cannot leave you without a warrior."

"This child of ours would prefer a father who is alive to a father who has been tomahawked by her own people!"

"And where would I go? I cannot go to the fort."

"You must return to Pendleton in South Carolina where you formerly lived. Attakullakulla has discussed it with me. You will be safe there. You will leave at sunrise tomorrow. You can wait no longer."

"Then come with me. You and Betsy and Short Fellow and Catherine and Tame Doe. You will live with me."

Nanyehi was silent for a moment. Then she said softly, "This I cannot do, Bryant. This I will never do. My place is with my people. You will return when these matters are settled, and we will be a family again."

But even as she spoke, she heard the doubt in her voice.

The next morning, Nanyehi sadly watched as Bryant loaded two packhorses, mounted his horse, and disappeared into the mist of the mountains. She confided to her mother, "I do not know if things will ever be the same. We may never be able to live as we once did."

The white chiefs sent Colonel Montgomery to free the captives of the fort, but they were defeated by Oconostota and his warriors. The siege of Fort Loudoun, which had begun in the spring rains, continued then through the long, hot days of summer. Beloved Mother announced her plan to Attakullakulla one day late in summer.

"Tomorrow I leave for Fort Loudoun. I will travel with Yellow Star and Red Bird, who have white husbands in the fort. They are anxious to see their husbands. We have heard that those inside are now starving. I will see what can be done."

When Nanyehi and Yellow Star and Red Bird arrived near the fort, they went straight to the camp of Willenawah. Nanyehi announced her intentions to the chief.

"These two," said Nanyehi, "they will speak with their husbands. The Unakas will be persuaded to surrender."

"This will not be, Ghigau," Willenawah warned. "They cannot go into the fort. They will try to take provisions and will inform those inside of our position."

"No matter! We will go!" It was Yellow Star who spoke defiantly. She had packed a bag of beans and pork and had hidden them under her blanket.

"I know these two," said Nanyehi. "They will ride to the gate even if you threaten to shoot them. Let them go. It will be better this way. They will tell the white people that our warriors are prepared to spend long days in the siege. They will tell them that the white king will send no more warriors to their aid and soon they will all die of starvation."

Nanyehi motioned for the two women that they should ride on. Willenawah would have it that they not go, but still he knew that the Beloved Woman of Chota usually got her way, and so he watched as the two women rode off. But when the sun had met the darkness in the horizon, his angry words burst upon her. "Why have I listened to you? The white men are even now plotting their escape."

Early the next morning, however, when the mist was still resting in the low places, the warriors wakened their chief. "They are coming!" the warriors announced. "Two soldiers ride with them. One of them carries the white flag."

So Oconostota allowed them to ride into his camp, and he accepted the white flag of truce. But his words to the men were sharp: "You will be allowed to leave and journey to a place of white settlement safely, if you can abide by our rules. We will allow you to take food, guns, and ammunition. But you must take only that which you need to secure a safe passage to your land. The rest will be left for our use."

Oconostota and a large band of his warriors traveled that first day with the white soldiers that they might have safe passage through the land.

Now after the group had left, Nanyehi went with the remaining

Ani-Yunwiya warriors into the fort to gather the food and ammunition left behind. When they came to the stone fortress, where the cannon and other guns were stored, they could hardly believe what they saw before them.

"It is all gone!" Nanyehi exclaimed. "What has happened?"

"The Unakas are deceivers!" declared Dragging Canoe. "When will we learn that they cannot be trusted?"

The warriors searched the area and found that the guns and ammunition and also the cannon had been thrown into the river, so that they could not be used by the Indians, and thus the agreement was broken.

"I will ride out now and inform Oconostota of these happenings," declared Dragging Canoe.

Nanyehi stepped forward and cut him off before he could mount his horse. She looked him squarely in the eye and said, "Cousin, see that nothing foolish is done!"

But his reply was sharp. "Cousin, the foolishness has already been done!"

When Dragging Canoe and Oconostota returned the next day, Nanyehi knew that what she feared most had taken place. Oconostota gathered together his warriors and informed them of his actions.

"We would have allowed the Unakas to depart and would not even have asked for the vengeance that was our due because of the murder of our twenty-eight chiefs. But the Unakas have broken their agreement again, and for this we have taken the lives of twenty-eight of their warriors! Now we may rest because the blood of our chiefs has been avenged."

Nanyehi returned to Chota where she informed Attakullakulla of the sad events. Attakullakulla was devastated. "It was I who was in favor of the building of Fort Loudoun," he said. "And what has become of it? Sometimes I do not know my place in the world."

A few days later, Nanyehi again approached Attakullakulla. "I am sorry to bring you more bad news, Uncle," she began. "Bryant sends word that the white war party is soon on its way. Colonel Grant is on march with two thousand troops of warriors. They will not rest until their disgrace has been avenged. Every town of the Ani-Yunwiya is in danger."

Wearily, Attakullakulla made plans again to meet with white officials to see that this matter might be settled peaceably. When he arrived at Fort Prince George, he was granted a conference with Colonel Grant.

"I am, and have been, a great friend to the English. I have been called an old woman by my own people for this. The conduct of my warriors has filled me with shame, however, and I would intercede on their behalf."

Attakullakulla's pleas for his people were not heard. The white soldiers marched against the towns of the Ani-Yunwiya, destroying fifteen towns and fifteen hundred acres of crops. Five thousand of our people were driven from their homes and fled to the refuge of the hills.

The Ani-Yunwiya fought a brave resistance, but they could not survive without the supplies of guns and ammunition from the British.

The town of Chota had not been attacked, but news of the destruction soon reached the ears of Nanyehi and Attakullakulla, who were quick to mount their horses and ride out.

They first approached the town of Etchoe. There they saw that all had been destroyed. The beans and peas and corn had been pulled up. The houses had been burned. The horses and pigs had been slaughtered. The people were gone. There was only one person there. He was a young boy of perhaps twelve years.

Nanyehi called to him, "Where are the people?"

"They are still hiding in the mountains. I have come to see if any food is left, for we all are starving. We only have roots and small animals to supply us. Many are sick. Many have died."

At the towns of Neowee and Kanuga, Nanyehi and Attakullakulla saw the same things.

"Let us return," said Nanyehi. "I can look at no more. We will send others back with provisions."

"The strength of the white man is great. We will win no more battles against him," predicted Attakullakulla.

"There must be no more wars with the white man! We must learn his ways, and we must learn to live peacefully with him!" declared Nanyehi. "It is our only hope as a nation."

CHAPTER 12
The Way of the Wolf

When Attakullakulla and Nanyehi arrived in Chota, they found that Attakullakulla had been summoned by Governor Bull to attend the peace treaty meeting. Nanyehi thought to accompany him, so that she might speak with the white chiefs also, but Attakullakulla discouraged her.

"It is a strange thing, Nanyehi, but women do not attend the council meetings of the white people. The white fathers do not allow it."

"How can this be?" asked Nanyehi incredulously.

"I myself have put that question to them," replied Attakullakulla. "At the first council meeting I attended I asked the white chiefs, 'Is not the white man also born of a woman?' I was told that the matter of ruling and decisions is a matter for men only."

Nanyehi stomped her foot. "It is only when mothers, wives, and daughters attend such meetings that there will be fewer wars and longer times of peace."

But she did not argue further with Attakullakulla, and she busied herself with gathering aid for the stricken villages. Thus it was that Attakullakulla attended the peace conference with other chiefs and warriors, but without Nanyehi.

Attakullakulla returned in the coldest month of winter in the year of 1761 with the documents of the agreement. He called his people together in council.

"I have sat with our white brothers in council. We have smoked the peace pipe. The War of the Cherokee and the English has ended. I have told my white brothers that as we all live in one land, we shall live as one people. The knot of friendship is between us again. Your Beloved Woman would now address you."

Nanyehi then arose and looked out to her people. She chose her words carefully:

"Brothers and Sisters of the Ani-Yunwiya, I have seen with my own eyes the results of our recent war with the British. Many of our bravest warriors are now dead. We have no more ammunition. Fifteen of our towns were destroyed. The houses were burned, the crops pulled up, the animals killed. Our people escaped to the mountains, but they are without provisions, and many are sick and dying.

"Listen to my words! The British are a powerful and superior force. Their knowledge and their ways of war are beyond ours. They grow in numbers every day. They will not be driven out! We must learn their ways. It is not every Unaka who would be our enemy. Many of them would be our friends. We must know these people and let them be of good use to us."

Nanyehi knew to be careful in how she spoke, for there were many who still believed that the Ani-Yunwiya must return to their former ways to be strong and to repel the advancing white man. So she said little else but went about as an example to her people, for she herself had large fields of crops, a herd of pigs, and a small band of horses. These she raised and traded to the white men in exchange for iron cooking utensils, rifles and ammunition, and cloths for making soft clothes. Her two daughters, Catherine and Elizabeth, were instructed in both the way of the Unaka and the way of the Ani-Yunwiya. Her son, Short Fellow, learned the way of the warrior and also the way of the manager of land and trade.

Now many saw that Beloved Mother did well and sought to be like her, but many others feared the loss of the Ani-Yunwiya ways.

It was Short Fellow who came forward and told her the remarks of the children: "Mother, the others say that you would have all of us be as white people. They tease us and call us 'Unaka.'"

Beloved Mother thought on this for a minute, and then she took Short Fellow upon her knee and spoke gently to him:

"Short Fellow, you know we are of the wolf clan. It has been the way of our ancestors to learn the way of the wolf, our blood brother of the mountains. We have seen how our brother, the wolf, can live in the depths of the swamp or in the coldest parts of the highest mountain, for he learns to adjust himself to whatever surrounds him. Thus he is revered by our people, for he is a creature who will survive. We, as a people, must learn from the knowledge of the wolf. We must adjust ourselves to our changing world if we are to survive as a people. So you see even today, you and I, we are living by the teachings of our people."

Beloved Mother then called her other two children, Catherine and Betsy, and she took all three of them outside to a nearby tree. She plucked a leaf.

"See this leaf? It can only live on the tree. If you pluck it and hold it out like this, it drifts to the ground, where it will soon turn brown and die."

Then she pointed to a bird roosting in the tree. "Watch this one as he proceeds in flight from the tree."

She shook the tree then, and the bird flew out from the branches and soared in the sky overhead.

"See how he flies? While he is in flight, he is always alert to the patterns of the wind. He changes his feathers and the position of his wings to better glide and proceed through the air. We must be as the bird. We must be alert to the changes in the winds around us and position ourselves that we may glide through life as the bird does."

Now as she spoke with her children, she heard a voice calling to her from across the field.

"Mrs. Ward? Are you Nancy Ward?"

Beloved Mother turned to see a young man with hair the color of blazing fire coming towards her. She noted his walk and his smile and the way he carried his gun, and she knew who he was.

"You are Jack, am I not right? Son of my husband, Bryant Ward?" she asked.

"I am. I arrived in Charles Town from Ireland and came to find my father. I am told that he lives in your nation."

"It has been some time that your father moved from our home. He now resides in the Pendleton District of South Carolina. He comes from time to time to visit, and we ourselves have just returned from a visit to his home."

She put her arms around Betsy and said, "This is Betsy, your sister. She knows English well enough to understand you, but she is shy about speaking. Betsy, this is Jack. He is your brother. He has come from his mother's village across the great water."

Betsy stared with rounded eyes at her new brother, and she wound her arms around her mother's legs. Catherine and Short Fellow also stood awkwardly until Jack took a harmonica from his pack and began playing for them an Irish tune.

He then handed it to Short Fellow, who blew into it and laughed and clapped at the noise he had made. The other two then also took a turn.

Nanyehi again addressed her stepson. "You will stay with us for a while, yes? It would be a treat for Betsy and my other children to get to know you. They love to hear Bryant's stories of life across the big water."

Jack Ward stayed for a full moon. He entertained the children with stories. He played many Irish songs for them on his harmonica, and he also sang Irish lullabies. The children, in turn, showed him their dances. Short Fellow showed him how to use the blow dart to kill a bird. And with the help of Tame Doe, the girls baked corn bread and wove a splendid basket for their guest.

When it came time for him to journey on to visit his father, Nanyehi reminded him that he was always welcome in their home.

"Will not Father return to live again now that the days of war are over?"

"It is not such an easy matter. Things are not the same as they once were. There are more white men on the frontier. There are now trading posts and forts, and not so many of the traders live in our villages. Bryant would that we live with him. But this cannot be, as my people are much in need at this time."

Jack Ward, like his father, came to love the people of Chota. He returned to make his home in that area. He married Katie McDaniel, whose father was a Scotchman and whose mother was a full-blood.

CHAPTER 13
The Voice of Dragging Canoe

It was as Beloved Mother had told young Jack Ward—the white man had extended his settlements so that there were now cabins near the Cherokee villages. When the Ani-Yunwiya protested, King George drew a proclamation line along the Blue Ridge Mountains to assure them of their hunting ground. But it was not long before the white settlers had crossed this line and would not be removed.

The people of the Watauga settlement determined a way that they might appease the Cherokee. They sent representatives with gifts of whiskey, guns, and trinkets to counsel with the chiefs. These men made speeches that were full of praise for their Cherokee brothers. They proposed a lease agreement by which the Cherokee could keep the ownership of their land. Even Henry Stuart, Deputy Indian Superintendent, was persuaded by their talks.

Only Dragging Canoe attempted to discourage the agreement.

"We should not give in on this matter," he warned his people. "It is our land, and the white fathers should force them to move off."

But when the official vote was taken, the lease agreement was favored by a majority. Attakullakulla sent word to the agent, Henry Stuart: "Father, I will eat and drink with my white brothers and will expect friendship from them. It is only a little spot of ground they seek, and I am willing that they should have it. I pity the white people, but they do not pity me. The Great Being above is very good. He provides for all. He gave us this land, but the white people want to drive us from it."

The Unakas thus determined that it was possible to negotiate for land, and they became more and more bold and more and more eager to acquire larger tracts of land, so that in the years that followed, much of the Cherokee land was sold.

On a spring morning in the white man's year of 1775, as Beloved Mother was heading to check the fields for planting, she was startled by the noise of activity from the village. She turned her horse and rode in to Chota. The dogs were barking loudly, and the people had gathered in the open spaces between the houses. The children were running out to the edge of town, pointing at the wagons in the distance and calling to their parents to come see what was soon to be in their midst.

Beloved Mother looked into the distance and saw a great caravan of wagons. It was of such a great length that it could have been wrapped around the entire village. She urged her horse forward and rode out to meet these travelers.

A band of white men was riding with the caravan, but Nanyehi did not recognize any of them. She approached the one who seemed to be in charge, and she identified herself. "I am Nancy Ward of Chota. What is your purpose?"

"Greetings, Nancy. I have heard of you. I am Richard Henderson. I have come to speak with Attakullakulla and your other chiefs. My company would buy lands from you in Tennessee and Kentucky, and we would pay you with these goods," he said as he gestured to the wagons. He then proceeded to several of the wagons and pulled off the top cloth, and she could see that the wagons were filled with guns, ammunition, clothing, blankets, mirrors, iron tomahawks, knives, and trinkets.

Beloved Mother conducted the head men of this group to the council house. They spoke with Attakullakulla, and he made arrangements to meet with them in council. He also sent messages to other villages that their chiefs might be present. On the day of the talks, many chiefs were gathered. Attakullakulla, Oconostota, The Raven, Old Abram, The Tassel, Hanging Maw, and Bloody Fellow sat on one side as the respected older chiefs. Next to them was seated Nanyehi in her position as Beloved Woman. The younger chiefs—

Willenawah the Great Eagle, Tanasi Warrior, Tuckasee the Terrapin, and Dragging Canoe—sat on the other side.

Richard Henderson had a large box filled with whiskey. He brought out the bottles and passed them around so that all of the chiefs and warriors might have their fill. Now many spoke in favor of the land sale. Their stomachs were full of the whiskey, their ears were full of the praises of the white men gathered, and their eyes were turned to the wagons filled with goods. But there were also those who would not sell more land.

Dragging Canoe rose to speak for them. Nanyehi looked upon her cousin. He was now a middle-aged man, a chief by virtue of his leadership powers. He was tall—over six feet. His frame was powerful and his voice was commanding.

"Brothers and Sisters," he began, "think on these things the Unakas ask us to do today. And think also of our dealings with the Unakas in the past.

"We were, at the time of my childhood, a great and powerful nation. We laid claim to vast areas of land. Our hunters could pursue with confidence the game on our land. Our women tended our homes, and our children lived without fear of loss of supplies. This is no longer so.

"The Unakas have moved upon our land. They have bought large areas of our land for trinkets and supplies which are now gone. When we would not sell the land, they took it anyway, and they made war with us and demanded it by right of peace treaty. They will continue to do this until they have taken all of our land and have forced us to move west to the other side of the Big River.

"I say we put a stop to the sale of our lands now! We must hold to our land if we are to remain the Ani-Yunwiya."

Nanyehi could see that many of the people were stirred by the speech of Dragging Canoe, but still the effect of the good whiskey and the food and the lure of the loaded wagons was strong. When the vote was taken, the land purchase was approved.

But Dragging Canoe could then no longer speak with a restrained voice. His words burst forth angrily at the signing ceremony.

"These treaties are only for men who are too old to hunt or fight! As for me, I have my warriors, and I will fight for my land! I will speak no more of treaties."

He then turned and faced the white men seated before him. "You will find that the land you want has a cloud hanging over it, and the settlement you speak of will be a dark and bloody one!"

Angrily he stalked from the council house. Many of the young warriors followed him.

Nanyehi remained seated with the older chiefs until the final papers had been signed. But then she hurried to her home and sent for Tomi that he might take a message to Dragging Canoe. "Tell him that I invite him to dine with myself and Attakullakulla this evening. Tell him we will discuss these matters that we might all be in agreement for the peace of our people."

But Dragging Canoe would not come—he sent a message in return: "The time for talk has now ended. I will be busy with the work of defending my people from the further encroachments of deceitful white men."

CHAPTER 14
The Words of Warning

In the months that followed, Nanyehi saw little of Dragging Canoe. He came no more to her house, nor did he go to the home of Attakullakulla. Nanyehi heard rumors that he traveled to the lower settlements to speak with the more warlike elements of the Ani-Yunwiya.

The Ani-Yunwiya were not the only people unhappy with their treatment by the whites. The Indian tribes across the eastern part of the country had been meeting and having talks. They might not be able to repress the white advances as individual tribes, but if they acted together, surely, they could overcome.

So it happened that on a warm spring day, Betsy came bounding into the cabin calling loudly, "Mother! Mother! Come quickly! Many chiefs have come! They are now at the council house! Some with long braids! Many with eagle feathers! Hurry! Come! What could be their purpose?"

When Nanyehi arrived at the council house, she saw that chiefs representing fourteen tribes had come to Chota. Already Attakullakulla was there in discussion with them. Nanyehi was surprised to see Dragging Canoe approaching the council house also.

She called to him, "Welcome, Cousin. It has been a long time since I have seen you. What business keeps you from my company for so long?"

"You know, Nanyehi, that I have made it my business to see that we are not taken advantage of by the whites. I have gone to seek support from those who agree with me."

He then stepped closer to Nanyehi and looked earnestly into her face.

"The chiefs who are here today—they are a delegation of Northern tribes. They are Iroquois, Mohawk, Delaware, Ottawa, Nantucas, Shawnee, and Mingo. They would join forces with us. Their talks are known throughout the Southeast.

"This is our chance, Nanyehi! This is our chance to be heard by the white man. They will see that the native people of the land can stand as one power against them. If they cannot abide by our words, then they will be driven out!"

Nanyehi took a step back, and she looked squarely at her cousin.

"I will hear their words, Dragging Canoe. But the day has passed when we, or any other people, would be able to drive the white man out. They are too numerous and too powerful."

Attakullakulla and Oconostota sent word to all of the Ani-Yunwiya villages that all might send representatives to the "Grand Talks." On the appointed day, they gathered in the council house.

The visiting chiefs rose one by one and told of their suffering at the hands of the white men. It was Cornstalk, the great chief of the Shawnee, who made the final speech:

"The Shawnee were once a great nation that hunted on land that stretched to the seashore. We have been reduced to a handful of people with only enough ground to stand upon. It appears that the white man intends to totally destroy the red people. It would be better for us to die like warriors than to be slowly pushed into our graves. Our cause is just! Surely the Great Spirit will see this and come to our aid!"

The great chiefs then came forward, one by one, and offered their war belts to the Ani-Yunwiya as symbol of their willingness to fight as one. Cornstalk was the last; his belt was of purple color, over nine feet long and six inches wide. He had poured red vermillion over one side to represent the blood of war.

Nanyehi tensed as she studied the faces of the chiefs. The pause of heavy silence was broken when Dragging Canoe stepped forward to accept the belt of Cornstalk. Then Osioota, a warrior chief from Chilhowie, arose and took his tomahawk and struck the war pole. Other Cherokee warriors came forward then, too. They held the war belt over their heads as they began to chant the ancient war song. Other Ani-Yunwiya braves rose and joined them. The musicians began to beat on the drums, and others picked up the rattling gourds. Soon nearly all the warriors in the council house had joined in the frenzied activity.

Nanyehi looked at the older chiefs. They sat silently and rigidly. If they would not speak, she decided, then she must make her own voice be heard. She would remind her warriors of their sufferings in the last war with the British. But as she looked about, she knew that the motions of war were now in progress, and she knew that her words would not be heard.

Attakullakulla then leaned toward her and said, "The white traders in the village are no longer safe. I fear for their lives. At the first opportune moment, Nanyehi, break away and make haste to their cabin that you might warn them."

When the crowd began dispersing, Nanyehi left the council house and headed in the direction of her own lodge. She had only taken ten steps when she heard the voice of Dragging Canoe calling to her. "Where do you go at such an early hour, Nanyehi?"

She turned and calmly answered, "Mother is not well, Dragging Canoe. Betsy has sent word that I must come at once."

And she proceeded on as if she were in a great hurry.

Now when she had gone far enough, and she knew that her form was no longer visible, she turned and headed toward the cabin of the white traders.

All was dark when she reached it. She knocked on the door and called out softly, "It is only I, Nancy Ward." But still there was no answer. She pushed the door in gently, but no one was inside. She could see by the moonlight coming in through the cabin windows that their blankets and guns were no longer there.

"That is good," she thought. "Already they are on their way. Perhaps they are safely past our borders."

She then hastened to her own cabin. She was surprised to see that all was dark there, too. Where was Tame Doe? Had she already extinguished the lantern and the fire? Had Betsy not returned from the activities in town? Her other children, Catherine and Short Fellow, were now living on their own, so it was only Tame Doe and Betsy who should have been there.

As she came closer to the porch, she made out the form of her daughter Betsy running toward her.

"Mother, they are here!" she said breathlessly when she was close enough. "Inside. The white traders. They came and asked to be let in. They said their lives were in danger. I let them in. Did I do the right thing?"

"You did well, Betsy. We will see to this matter."

Nanyehi entered her cabin to see that before her sat Isaac Thomas, Jarrett Williams, and William Fawley.

"We are sorry, Nancy. We hope that we did not frighten you or your family. We were on our way into the settlement from a hunting trip when we heard the war whoops and saw the war poles painted black. We knew it was not safe to return to our own cabin then, so we made our way along the stream to your cabin. Your mother has given us food, and we will now be on our way."

"No! It is not safe now. Wait until tomorrow evening. Tonight the warriors are roused and would be apt to do something dangerous and foolish. I fear for your lives. Tomorrow we begin the formal preparations for war. Our leaders and warriors will be thus engaged, and they will think that you have already been gone for a long time."

The sound of approaching hoofbeats broke Nanyehi's speech. Betsy ran to the window and called back to them, "It is Dragging Canoe! What will we do?"

Nanyehi rose and looked quickly about her. "Everyone will stay in here. I will step out and talk with him."

She stepped quickly outside as Dragging Canoe dismounted.

"So?" she began. "You have finally come to honor me with a visit. It is late for talks, Dragging Canoe. Mother is still not well, and she has just now fallen asleep. I would that we not go in for fear that we will wake her."

Dragging Canoe looked from right to left and then straight ahead to the cabin behind his cousin. Satisfied that no one was there, he spoke softly. "Tomorrow, we meet, Ghigau, to begin the official rites of war. Be at the council house at sunrise for the preparation of the black drink."

Again Dragging Canoe looked from right to left, then he strained forward and this time spoke more sharply to his cousin.

"We are at war, Nanyehi. The white men are our brothers no longer! I hope I do not need to remind you of where your loyalties lie."

"We would not all be at war, Dragging Canoe. My loyalties have always been with my people. I hope I do not need to remind you that we must always walk the path that is best for our people, and not just the path that pleases our angry feelings."

Dragging Canoe said nothing. Nanyehi then bid him farewell. "I will see you in the morning, Dragging Canoe."

Early the next morning Nanyehi arose and instructed the traders: "I go to begin the ceremonies for war, as is my duty as Ghigau. Stay through the light of day. When I return tonight, I will inform you of the dangers that lie ahead."

As Nanyehi approached the council house, she saw Dragging Canoe talking with the English agent, Henry Stuart. Dragging Canoe's face was painted with the red and black of war. She hastened forward that she might hear his speech.

Dragging Canoe's voice was angry and demanding. "Where have the white traders gone? Why are they no longer in the village? Why are you yourself making preparations to depart?"

"The traders are gone because they fear for their lives," answered

Henry Stuart. "They have hidden in the woods. This war that you wage, Dragging Canoe, will be destructive to your own people. I cannot remain and be associated with it. I have urged you to wait upon the British government. They are now themselves at war with the white settlers who want their independence. They would come to your aid if you would wait. But you have not listened to my advice."

"We have waited long enough. The writing of letters and the signing of treaties has only lost us more land. I, myself, have decided to take charge of these things and not leave the fate of our people in the hands of other white men. The time is now right! We will push the whites off of our lands forever!"

Stuart shook his head sadly. "This war you begin will be the destruction of the Cherokee nation. Take care that at least you do not harm women or children or take the lives of those who are loyal to our king."

The words of Henry Stuart echoed in Nanyehi's mind as she entered the council house. Another war with the whites could very well bring destruction to her people.

Now Beloved Mother was dressed in her ceremonial clothes—her white buckskin dress and beaded moccasins and her cape of swan wings. She approached the fire in the center of the council house and saw that already the pots of simmering water were waiting. The council house grew quiet as she assumed the correct posture and looked to Dragging Canoe, who was now acting as the war chief. Dragging Canoe nodded, and she then withdrew from her pouch the leaves of the yaupon and held them in her cupped hands. She looked upward and murmured the ritual prayer. She then sprinkled some of the leaves into each of the pots and threw the rest at the feet of Dragging Canoe. She waved the swan's wing over the brewing mixture and then sat down near the fire.

She looked about at the warriors gathered. They could now begin their talks while they waited for the black drink to brew. While she sat thus, watching the steam rise from the pots, she suddenly gasped, for she saw in the rising mist the faces of the Ani-Yunwiya children, warriors, and mothers who had died as a result of the last war with the whites. Their faces were contorted in pain and their forms cried out silently to her.

She looked at the braves seated, but they were in discussion and seemed to pay no attention to her. That was good, for she did not want them to see the trembling of her limbs.

Her mind, though, was screaming the pain she felt: "What am I to do? What am I to do? I cannot let this happen! How can I possibly stop it?"

She looked at the fire then, and silently she projected her prayer, "Carry my petitions to the Great Spirit above. Guide my actions. Show me what is to be done." She watched as the smoke rose from the fire, carrying her petitions upward.

She sat quietly and waited for an answer. When she judged the mixture was of the appropriate strength, she picked up the conch shell, dipped it into the largest pot, and offered the first drink to Dragging Canoe. He drank from it and passed it on to the other warriors. They would continue to sip from the black drink as the day progressed, abstaining from any other food or drink. The black drink assured them that they would be purged of all wrong thoughts or actions committed in the past. The Spirits above would then see their good intentions and would come to their aid in battle.

Nanyehi remained throughout the day, waiting upon them and keeping the pots replenished with the black liquid. As the time passed, her spirit was eased, for she knew then what she was to do. She could not stop the war which had even now begun, but she could take steps to minimize the loss of life for both sides.

At nightfall she returned to her own lodging. The three traders were waiting, their belongings packed and their horses ready.

"It is good that you leave tonight," Nanyehi began. "Our warriors will observe two more days of fasting and preparation. The attack will begin soon after that. You must go to your villages and forts and warn your people. Tell your leaders that not all our chiefs nor all our people are behind these warriors. Tell them that many of us still want peace, that we would live with the white man as our brother. Many of us have children and family in the white settlements. My own daughter Catherine lives with her white husband near the white man's settlement.

"Travel the way of the river. I will send Tomi and his son to follow on their horses so that your tracks may be hidden with theirs. When you get to the river, Tomi will turn back. Our friend Henry Stuart has left today also. Perhaps you will meet up with him. Inform him of my concern. Perhaps he will be able to do something more for us."

The traders safely departed, and Nanyehi returned to the council house the next morning to continue in the ceremonies.

On the fourth morning the people of the village gathered in the council square to send off their departing warriors. The warriors left in the midst of much whooping and shouting. As they approached the foot of the mountain in the distance, they broke into three groups. Dragging Canoe headed with his party to the settlements of South Virginia and Long Island on the Holston River. Chief Old Abram would lead a band against the settlements of Nolichucky and Watauga. The Raven was to lead his force against the western settlements of Carter's Valley.

The next few weeks went slowly by. Nanyehi went about her daily activities, tending her summer crops and preserving food for the winter months ahead. She and Tomi began the repair of the cabin and saw to it that the fences were all mended. The peaches could soon be picked, and they watched for the signs of ripeness every day.

Every evening Nanyehi put her prayers to the fire. She prayed for the safety of her own people, for the safety of the white people, and especially for the safety of her own son. Short Fellow had ridden out with the troops of Dragging Canoe. She had tried to discourage him, but Long Fellow, her brother, had interceded for his nephew.

"He is now a man, Nanyehi. He must do what every Ani-Yun-wiya warrior has done before. Do I need to remind you of your own decision to go to battle when you were his age?"

"But times are different now," protested Nanyehi. "The white man is much more powerful than our people."

"War is always the same, Nanyehi, as is the quest of the young for manhood. You must accept his decision."

Nanyehi knew her brother to be of the right mind. It did not make it easier, though, and she continued to pray each night for his safe return.

The news began to slowly trickle in. Although the Ani-Yunwiya were suffering humiliating defeat, Nanyehi felt encouraged by the news. The casualties for both sides had been few. The message of attack had reached the white settlements before the warriors did, and the whites were ready and waiting in each instance. Dragging Canoe was wounded in battle, and when he fell, his warriors gathered up their wounded and quickly retreated.

Chief Old Abram entered the Watauga area and found that the settlers had fled to the forts. When he sent his warriors to attack the fort, they were driven back by boiling pots of water that the women poured upon them.

The Raven, likewise, found the settlements in Carter's Valley abandoned. The people had gone to forts or retreated to the larger towns in Virginia.

Nanyehi and Attakullakulla met daily during this time to discuss the news brought to them by the messengers.

"Let us hope that Dragging Canoe will see that it is no easy matter to fight the white man. Perhaps he will now be eager to speak of peace," said Nanyehi.

"Let us hope that the white men will not judge our people too harshly. We can only wait to see what retribution will be taken," replied Attakullakulla.

CHAPTER 15
The Rescue of Lydia Bean

Attakullakulla and Nanyehi were still in her lodge discussing Dragging Canoe's defeat when they heard someone shouting from outside.

"Ghigau! Ghigau! Help! Come quickly!"

Beloved Mother arose and went out the door and into the yard. There, breathless before her, was Red Bird, daughter of her friend Yellow Bird, from the nearby town of Toqua.

"What is it, Red Bird?"

"They have a Unaka woman tied to the stake!"

"Where? Where, Red Bird, where?"

"In Toqua, Ghigau. Old Abram's warriors have her!"

Nanyehi waited to hear no more. She called to Tomi, "Bring out our horses! You will ride with us, Tomi!"

Red Bird continued to talk, pausing for gasps of air. "They will torture her first. If we hurry, we can save her from the fire."

"Wait here!" instructed Nanyehi. "I will get my things."

She returned with her cape of swan wings. Tomi was there with the horses. They mounted and quickly rode out. From the broken conversation on the ride to Toqua, Beloved Mother learned the rest of the story. Chief Old Abram's warriors had been humiliated by their defeat at the Watauga fort. The women had repelled them by pouring pots of boiling water down the walls of the stockade. Delayed when she tried to drive in a cow tethered outside, the white woman had not made it in time—the stockade gate had been closed to her.

As Beloved Mother, Tomi, and Red Bird approached the town of Toqua, they heard the shouts of the warriors near the river. They urged the horses forward in that direction.

The Unaka woman was tethered to the stake in the middle of the group. Her eyes were closed; her face was distorted with anguish. Dry tree branches and twigs were scattered over a large area around the pole. Already the warriors had begun to light the branches furthermost from the woman. The braves danced around the area, taunting the woman with their cries and war whoops.

As Beloved Mother approached the group, those on the outside ceased their movements. A murmur spread among them, "It is Ghigau. She carries the swan wings." They all knew that the wave of a swan's wing by a beloved woman of the tribe signified that the prisoner would go free. The white woman opened her eyes when she realized that all were now quiet.

Beloved Mother stood silently until all motion had ceased, then she kicked the larger burning branches away and stomped out the smaller flames. She approached the mound and cut the thongs, freeing the Unaka woman. Tomi gathered the trembling woman in his arms and carried her out to the side, where he laid her in the grass and gave her sips of water.

Beloved Mother turned to the group of warriors. Her words rang out clearly:

"It revolts my soul to see such actions by Ani-Yunwiya warriors! As long as I am Ghigau, no woman will ever be tortured or burned at the stake. Now be gone, and may I never hear of such an incident again!"

Some of the warriors stepped forward, as if to challenge her. But others in the group pulled them back.

"Do you not know who this is?" one asked. "It is Ghigau from Chota. She is called Nanyehi, and it is said she walks with the Spirit People."

"She is the one who as a young woman rallied our people in battle and drove back the Creeks," added another.

"They say the white wolf himself has spoken to her."

So the warriors stood back and watched as Beloved Mother mounted her horse. Tomi placed the white woman in front of Beloved Mother, and the group slowly rode off in the direction of Chota.

The ride to Chota was a quiet one. The white woman did not speak on the ride except to ask, "Where do you take me?"

"We go to my home in Chota," Nanyehi answered.

"A Cherokee town? How can I be safe in a Cherokee town?"

"You will be with me. I promise no more harm will come to you."

When they arrived in Chota, the people gathered around to see this white woman, but Beloved Mother sent them on their way. "You must let her be. She has been through a great ordeal. We must treat her kindly. She must rest."

For three days the white woman said nothing, but rested on a bed and drank only water and would have nothing to eat. On the fourth day she sat up and said to Beloved Mother, "It was because of the cow. We had tethered her outside the gate to graze. I insisted that I would have time to bring her in safely, but I did not. All for that cow!"

"You must have valued your cow," Beloved Mother said gently as she sat beside her. She waited a moment, and then she asked, "What are you called?"

The woman looked at her and answered, "I am Lydia Bean." She said it slowly as if she were discovering it herself for the very first time.

"Your husband then is William Bean?"

"Yes," she said and paused. Then she looked at Beloved Mother accusingly. "How did you know this?"

"He was the first settler in the Watauga District. I have often heard of him."

"Who are you? Wait . . . I know! You are Nancy Ward, wife of Bryant Ward, and a chieftainess of your tribe! Am I correct?"

"Yes."

"I have often heard of you."

Lydia Bean rose from her bed and walked out onto the porch. Beloved Mother followed her.

"This is all yours? The field of corn, the horses, the pigs? All of these buildings? What do you do with all of these buildings?"

"The house behind this one is for my slaves. The other houses are for hanging the meat and drying tobacco."

"You have slaves? Am I now also a slave?"

Beloved Mother smiled. "Do not worry. We will return you to your people when it may be safely done."

Lydia Bean turned to her and asked, "You have no cows?"

"Our people do not raise cows. We call them the white man's buffalo. It is believed that the meat of the cow will make one slow and sluggish. We do not eat the meat of the pig either. We only sell it to the white traders."

"But what about milk? Do not your children drink milk?"

"Of course they have their mother's milk as infants. What other milk would they have?"

"Our children drink cow's milk. Our doctors tell us it builds strong bones. We make butter and cheese from it also."

"I have heard of this. Perhaps our children would do well to have cow's milk."

"When do I return to my own people?"

"We will see. It will be when I can provide you with a safe escort. Too many of our warriors wish that you were dead and would gladly see that it is so."

"They are savages! I have seen how it is! Your warriors are savages! Why do you not leave these people yourself and live with your white husband?"

"Your warriors act as savages also. I have seen for myself how my people were treated in the last war. Our villages were burned; our warriors were killed and scalped. War is a savage business for both sides."

"But we only want to live in peace."

"You have taken our land to live upon. It is your people who invaded our land with no regard for the line drawn by the king."

At this Lydia Bean said nothing.

"We prepare for the Green Corn Festival. It is a sacred time for our people. After this, things will be safe enough for you to leave."

"What is this Green Corn Festival? It is a pagan rite! Will I be forced to participate?"

"You will not be asked to do anything you do not wish to do. Perhaps it is good that you are here at this time. You have seen some of the worst activities of my people. Now you will see also that we are a civilized people who strive to live in harmony with all."

But Lydia Bean's anger would not be quieted. "You do not realize it now," she said, "but the way of the white world is the best way. It was meant to be. Your people cannot continue with their ways."

"We will see. Have not our people been open to the ways of the white man? You see—we plow the fields, we spin cotton, we hunt with rifles. We have come to appreciate your ways. But the white man has had no respect for our ways. We are not the savages you believe us to be. Observe the ways of our Green Corn Festival—you will see that the way of the Ani-Yunwiya is the way of peace and harmony with the world about."

Beloved Mother turned then and quickly walked back to the house. Lydia Bean called after her, "I am sorry. I do not wish to offend you."

She hastened to catch up to Beloved Mother, and she asked, "What is the purpose of the Green Corn Festival?"

"The Festival is one of seven held throughout the year. It is at this time that we eat of the first new corn crop. It is the time of the new year when the disorder of our old lives is discarded, and we are all born anew.

"Already Attakullakulla, our peace chief, has sent messengers to the other villages. He has notified them that the green corn is ripe.

The messengers will return with seven ears of corn, one from each of our seven clans, for seven is the sacred number of the Ani-Yun-wiya. The chief and his counselors have begun the fast of seven days. On the last day our ceremonies will begin."

Lydia Bean watched as Beloved Mother readied her own household for the ceremony. Her cabin and all the surrounding buildings were cleaned and swept out. The old, broken pottery was discarded. The buildings were checked and the rotting places were mended. On the seventh day of the festival, Beloved Mother extinguished the fire in the hearth and took care to see that all of the ashes were removed.

The people of the village gathered at the river, where the adawehi led them in the purification rites. They waded out and faced the rising sun. The adawehi dipped each of them seven times under the running water. When this was done, he lifted his voice and loudly proclaimed, "Into the waters of Long Man River we have cast our impurities. We have risen from the water as a new people! We go forth in a state of perfection and harmony to begin our new lives."

All then went to the council house, where last year's fire had been extinguished. It was time now for the relighting of the sacred fire. Beloved Mother and Lydia Bean and all the gathered people watched as the fire-maker rekindled the fire. He rolled the stick rapidly between the palms of his hands until smoke and flames were produced in the tinder of the goldenrod blossoms. The feeble flame was then fed with seven different kinds of wood until it was a bright and strong fire.

The great peace chief, Attakullakulla, took the kernels from the ears of corn provided by the seven clans and placed them in the sacred fire. He offered this corn with a prayer of thanksgiving. He sprinkled powder made from tobacco over the fire also.

He then spoke out to his people. "We eat now of the corn of new life."

The women brought forward the food prepared from the new corn crop, and all of the people feasted. No one was allowed to eat any more of the corn from the last year's harvest.

As the women left the council house, they carried with them embers from the sacred fire that they might rekindle the fire in their own homes.

That evening the people gathered again at the council house for dancing and celebration. As the drums were beating and the people gathered around the dancers, Lydia Bean spoke to Beloved Mother. "The other parts of your ceremony, those I can understand. But the dances and the drums—these I do not understand. Your people appear as wild savages! It frightens me. I want to return to the house."

"Stay," Nanyehi answered her. "I will explain it to you. You will see that it all has meaning. The people now begin the Pheasant Dance."

Lydia Bean agreed then to stay for the moment, and Beloved Mother explained the meaning of the steps.

"The dancers beat the ground with their feet in imitation of the drumming sound made by the pheasant when he beats his wings. It is said that the pheasant once saw a woman beating corn in a wooden mortar. 'I would do that, too,' he insisted, and he went out into the woods and perched upon a hollow log and 'drummed' with his wings as is the way of the pheasant. The people heard him and believed that he really was beating the corn.

"See how the people form two circles? The men are on the inside, facing the women on the outer circle. The story is told that there once came a winter famine, and the birds were near starvation. It was then that a pheasant found a holly tree which was full of red berries. The holly berries are a favorite of the pheasant, so he called forward his companion birds, and they danced around the tree in a circle, drumming their wings in gratitude for the beautiful tree and the berries they found. Thus our musicians sing the pheasant song, and our dancers dance the pheasant's dance in honor of our own new-found crop of green corn, which will sustain us for the winter."

When the pheasant dance had ended, a young brave called out,

"Let us now do the Groundhog Dance!"

Another voice then shouted, "Long Arrow! Tell us first the story of the Groundhog Dance!"

Other cries then came from the group, "Yes! Tell us the story! We must have the story!"

Long Arrow nodded his assent, and the people gathered and sat around him. He waited until all was quiet, then he began, his voice ringing out clearly in the still night air.

"It happened that there were seven wolves who caught a groundhog. They said to him, 'Now we will kill you, and we will have something good to eat.'

"The groundhog was agreeable, but he reminded the wolves, 'When we find good food, you know we must rejoice over it, as the people do in the Green Corn Dance. Of course, I know you will kill me, and that this must be so; but before you do, I will teach you a dance, for it is an entirely new dance. I will even sing for you as you dance.'

"Now the wolves were very hungry, but they loved to dance, and so the groundhog's suggestion was agreeable to them.

"'I will lean up against seven trees in turn, and you will dance out and then turn and come back as I give the signal. At the very last turn, then you can kill and eat me.'

"The groundhog leaned up against the first tree and began his song. 'Ha´wiye´ehi´!' he called out. The line of wolves then danced out in front of him. When he gave the signal, 'Yu!' they turned and danced back in the other direction.

"'That is very good!' the groundhog praised them. 'I will now go to the second tree.'

"The groundhog leaned up against the second tree, and this time he sang out the song 'Hi´yagu´we!' and the wolves danced out again until he gave the signal 'Yu!' and they turned and danced back. And so the dance continued, with the groundhog complimenting the wolves after each tree on what a fine job they had done.

"With each tree, however, the groundhog came a little closer to his hole near a stump. At the seventh tree he said to the wolves, 'Now, here we are at the last dance. This time when I say "Yu," you will all turn and come after me. The first one who gets to me will then have me for a meal.'

"So it was that he began the seventh song. When the wolves had danced way out, he gave the signal 'Yu!' but then he turned and jumped for his hole, and he was in it before they could reach him.

"But he did not quite make a clean getaway, because the foremost wolf was able to catch hold of his tail, and he pulled on it so hard that it broke off. It is ever since then that the groundhog has had a very short tail."

The people then formed a line of dancers, and Beloved Mother and Lydia Bean watched as they danced out to the song of the musician who called out, "Ha´wiye´ehi!"

It was late into the night when Beloved Mother gathered her family and headed back to the cabin. The dancing and the singing were still continuing. When they were far enough from the council square to hear each other's words, Beloved Mother said to Lydia Bean, "I have counseled with Attakullakulla. It is agreed that tomorrow you will set out to return to your people. My own brother, Long Fellow, and my son, who is now called Five Killer, will accompany you on your journey."

"I thank you for my life, Nancy. I will remember your kindness and will tell my own people of the things that I have seen when I was with your people. I do not know how I can repay you."

"There is no need for repayment. We must use every opportunity we can to bring peace between our peoples. Perhaps our friendship will bring us closer to a lasting peace."

It was several weeks later that Five Killer and Long Fellow returned from their mission of returning Lydia Bean to the Watauga District. Beloved Mother was distressed at the lengthy delay.

"What takes them so long?" she complained to Betsy. "They must be stopping at every town and village to visit with old friends. Do they not know there is work to be done here?"

It was Betsy who spied them coming over the distant hill late one afternoon. She called out, "Mother, they are coming. Come see! No wonder it has taken them so long! They are bringing with them a cow and a calf."

Beloved Mother mounted her own horse and rode out to meet them.

Long Fellow protested to her, "A journey of three days has taken two weeks! The next time a friend sends a gift of gratitude, you must bring it home yourself."

But Beloved Mother was delighted, and she dismounted to examine her new charges. She walked slowly toward the cow and petted her behind the crown and crooned softly to the calf. Beloved Mother insisted that Long Fellow build a special shelter for the mother and calf.

She learned from the visiting white traders how to milk the cow and even how to make butter. Soon other women were demanding that they also have the "white man's buffalo."

CHAPTER 16
"Their Cry Is for More Land"

After the departure of Lydia Bean, Beloved Mother sent a message to Dragging Canoe: "My cry is all for peace. You see the white man, how he is much stronger. Let no more blood be shed. Let us be united to preserve our people."

But Dragging Canoe's response was not in agreement. "We are not yet defeated. We continue to fight. If we cannot win the white man's battle, then we will fight the Indian way."

Now the Indian way is to raid, loot, scalp, and be gone. So Dragging Canoe sent his warriors on a series of raids against the white settlements.

Beloved Mother met daily with Attakullakulla to discuss the news brought to them of the war on the frontier settlements. Black Hawk, Attakullakulla's trusted scout, arrived one day with grim news.

"They have killed a chief warrior in the white man's army. His name was Lieutenant Grant. Our scouts saw the remains of this man only three days ago. He was tied to a tree. His scalp and his ears had been cut off. A gun barrel had been thrust into his chest. Above him a bloody tomahawk was stuck in a tree. By now his own people will have found him."

Attakullakulla sadly shook his head. Beloved Mother rose and paced nervously about. Suddenly she stopped and cried out, "We will be destroyed! What is to be done now?"

But there was nothing to be done. The white government reacted by sending out forces full strength against the Cherokee, destroying thirty-six villages. When enough damage had been done, the chiefs were summoned to Long Island on the Holston River for a peace treaty. Attakullakulla and Nanyehi sent word to Dragging Canoe:

"Join us in the peace talks. The white man will totally destroy us if we do not come to an agreement. Only a few of our beloved towns still stand, and they are already overcrowded with refugees. There are not enough supplies to last the winter."

But Dragging Canoe's response was swift and decisive:

"My warriors and I will abandon our town on the Little Tennessee and move south to Chickamauga where we can operate free of the restraints of the white man. I urge all of you to abandon these talks of peace treaties and to join us."

So Chief Oconostota and Chief Attakullakulla attended the peace treaty without Dragging Canoe. But they were both now old, and so The Tassel went with them to serve as spokesman, and Nanyehi insisted that she go also.

The white commissioners began first by reproaching the chiefs for the raids committed in the Holston and Kentucky areas:

"Where are Dragging Canoe and those responsible? They must be made accountable for their crimes."

The Tassel responded, "These men have broken with our people and have now set up their own government and council at Chickamauga. We no longer have any influence over them. We can no longer be responsible for their actions."

The aged leaders of the Ani-Yunwiya were willing to sign the peace treaty, but they were saddened by the demands, for in so doing, they were forced to give up over five million acres of land.

"It is surprising that when we enter into treaties with our fathers, the white people, their whole cry is for more land." Nanyehi and the others heard the bitterness in the words of The Tassel as he addressed the white men. "It has become a formality with them to demand what they know we dare not refuse."

The Tassel then turned to directly face the white chiefs.

"What have you done? You marched into our towns with a far stronger force. Your numbers were well beyond ours. What did we do? We fled with our women and children to the sanctuary of the mountains. Our towns were left to your mercy. You killed the few defenseless ones left behind. Your fires destroyed our homes and crops, and you returned to your own dwellings well-pleased.

"You have made much of your attempts to bring 'civilization' to the red man. You have insisted that we adopt your laws, your religion, your manners, and your customs. You say, 'Why does not the red man till the ground and live as we do?' We ask, 'Why does not the white man hunt and live as we do?'

"Above all, however, we wish to be at peace with you. We would not quarrel with you for the killing of an occasional buffalo or deer on our lands, but your people go far beyond this. They hunt for trade. They kill all our game! And yet our braves are called criminals by your chiefs if they kill a cow or a hog to sustain them as they cross your lands.

"The Great Spirit has created us as two separate peoples. It is true he has given you many advantages, but he has not created us to be your slaves. Your land he has stocked with cows, hogs, and sheep; ours with bears, buffalo, and deer. Our animals are wild, but they are our property as other animals are yours. They should not be taken without our consent or unless exchanged for something of equal value."

The white commissioners were moved by the speech of The Tassel. They spoke among themselves and then replied, "Brother, your speech has been moving to us. We will amend the treaty so that the new line will be drawn further down the Nolichucky River."

After the signing of the treaty, a white soldier stepped forward and asked the Cherokees to join the American people in the celebration of a new government.

"Brothers, just one year ago the thirteen United States declared themselves free and independent of the British Crown. We Americans have been fighting the enemy, and we have killed thousands of them and have taken many prisoners. The Great Being above has seen our efforts and has made us prosperous. May this day and every day hereafter be a day of gladness. Brothers, on this day there is rejoicing throughout the thirteen united colonies from Canada to the Floridas. We hope our brothers, the Cherokee, will now rejoice with us."

The Tassel consulted with the old chiefs, then he turned and announced, "Brothers, we will celebrate your victory with you here today. Our warriors will perform the victory dance in honor of this day!"

The white soldiers then brought out bottles of whiskey and passed them around as the Ani-Yunwiya performed the celebration dance.

CHAPTER 17
"Our Cry Is All for Peace"

Nanyehi and the chiefs returned to Chota with the agreement of the peace treaty. But their return with words of peace was met with cries of war. The faces of the braves of Chota were painted red and black.

Nanyehi called on Black Hawk, trusted scout and advisor to Attakullakulla. "What is the meaning of this?" she questioned him.

"Ghigau, the British agents were here in your absence. They have promised supplies to us if we would fight against the Americans for the side of the British. They have promised that we can now have all of our land back!"

"Black Hawk, this will not be! I have seen the size and strength of the American army at the peace meetings. They will not lose this war. You will only bring more destruction upon us!"

But Black Hawk and the other braves ignored her counsel. They rode out the next day to join the troops of Dragging Canoe and others who fought for the British.

Attakullakulla and Nanyehi watched their departure with heavy hearts.

"Sometimes I think there is no such thing as peace, Uncle," said Nanyehi.

Attakullakulla agreed. "The way of our world is the way of war."

It was a few weeks later that Colonel Joseph Martin, Virginia's Superintendent of Indian Affairs, rode into Chota with news of the frontier war:

"Nancy, your warriors are being defeated by the American troops led by Colonel Campbell and Colonel Sevier. They are under orders to destroy all Cherokee villages."

"But not Chota!" protested Nanyehi. "They will not harm Chota. Chota is a city of refuge, a town of peace."

"They will destroy Chota also. You must prepare your people."

Nanyehi called her people together. "You must leave. Our warriors have been defeated. Colonel Martin tells us they will show no mercy. I will stay behind and see what peaceful arrangements can be made. I will send word when it is safe to return."

Nanyehi stayed to see that her people were on their way, but still she would not resign Chota to the fate that Colonel Martin predicted. As soon as all of her people had left, she mounted her horse and rode north along the river. She had only been riding for an hour when she spotted the camp of the white warriors.

As she approached, the soldiers drew their rifles and pointed them at her. But she did not look at their guns or at their faces. She rode forward, her gaze fixed straight ahead. She went to the largest tent in the center of the camp. A circle of soldiers was now around her, all of them with rifles pointed. She spoke to the man who stood outside of the tent. "I wish to speak with your chief warrior."

"That would be me!" A man exited the tent and stood before her. "I am Colonel Campbell."

"I am Nancy Ward."

"So you are." He then addressed the soldiers, "Gentlemen, be at ease. Mrs. Ward and I will be in discussion inside my tent."

Nanyehi did not wait for the Colonel to be seated before she began to speak.

"Colonel Campbell, our people would still be at peace with you. I beg you to consider our situation! We have been for months without supplies. My people have fled to the hills. Attakullakulla and Oconostota, our two great chiefs, are now old and unable to come themselves, but they would meet with you and discuss these terms of peace."

Colonel Campbell motioned for her to sit down before he answered.

"I would be at peace also, Nancy. My people and I are grateful to you for your kindnesses toward us in the past. I have heard of your rescue of Mrs. Bean and of your hiding the traders and sending them safely on their way. I promise that no harm will come to you or your family. These talks of peace, however, cannot be arranged until I have spoken with the warring parties of your people."

Nanyehi then knew that no more could be done. She mounted her horse and returned to Chota.

The next day the white soldiers entered the village. They gathered the stores of food. They pulled up what remained of the crops. They slaughtered the livestock and burned the houses.

Nanyehi stood in front of her cabin and watched all of these things, murmuring over and over to herself, "I cannot believe that they do this. Not to Chota! Not to our beloved town."

Tomi said to her, "Ghigau, come inside. It does no one good to watch these things. It will be harder to forget them." Beloved Mother then followed the counsel of Tomi and went into the the cabin. She stayed there until she heard the hoofbeats of horses near her own home and she heard her cattle stomping about and protesting with frightened noises.

She stepped outside then and saw two men rounding up her cows. "Who are you and what do you do with my cows?"

These two men looked at her, but did not answer. An officer then rode forward and said, "I am Colonel Clark. I am here by order of Colonel Sevier. We are not to harm you or your family or take any of your other stored supplies, but these animals are to be taken for slaughter. Our troops have no supplies, and soon they will be starving. We need these animals for food for our men."

"But you cannot have them!" insisted Nanyehi.

Still she knew there was nothing to be done, and she was nearly ready to go back in when she saw from the corner of her eye three men approaching. It was Colonel Martin and two of his own men.

"Good day, Colonel Clark," he said, addressing his fellow officer.

"Your services will not be needed here. I have already made arrangements with Mrs. Ward for the purchase of her cattle. She will be paid for them. My men will see that they are slaughtered and dressed for the troops."

"The hell you say!"

Beloved Mother was surprised at the angry response. Colonel Clark then spat on the ground and said under his breath, "Indian lover."

Then he looked up and said loudly, "I am under order from Colonel Sevier himself to deliver these animals to him! Now get your men out of my way!"

Colonel Martin only looked at him calmly and said, "I will not be sworn at, Colonel. I invite you to dismount so that we might discuss this matter in a civilized manner."

Both men then dismounted, but when they came face to face, Colonel Martin struck a blow to Colonel Clark so that he went reeling backward. He steadied himself, though, and came forward swinging with both fists. The fight continued until finally Colonel Clark was on the ground and could not get up. Colonel Martin then ordered his men to take possession of the animals, and he ordered Colonel Clark's men to leave.

Colonel Martin turned to Beloved Mother. "Nancy, I cannot save your animals from slaughter by American troops, but I can see that you are paid for them. I am sorry for this."

"I thank you, Colonel Martin."

"How is it with your people? How is your own family holding up?"

"My people have fled to the hills. Many are sick. Many more will starve, for now our winter supply has been destroyed.

"Only my family remains behind—Mother, Betsy, Attakullakulla, and also Oconostota. Attakullakulla is not well. I'm afraid his time is soon here. Mother is not well either. Oconostota seems strong enough, but he is nearly blind.

"Come in. Speak with Attakullakulla. He will be pleased to see that you have helped us."

The two of them went in to the back room where Attakullakulla was lying on his bed, his eyes closed. Tame Doe was kneeling at his side, her face hovering anxiously over his body, a string of red and black beads in her hands.

Nanyehi gasped when she first looked at them. Tame Doe looked up with a commanding expression and motioned that Nanyehi and Colonel Martin should depart.

They returned to the main room, and Nanyehi sat down quietly, burying her face in her hands.

"What is it, Nancy? He is dying, isn't he?" Colonel Martin asked.

Nanyehi looked up and said, "He is dead. Mother is saying the prayer of the departing spirit."

She turned to Tomi. "Ride out to the camp. Our people are a half day's ride to the south along the banks of the river. Tell them to return. Tell them the Unakas are gone. Tell them our chief, Attakullakulla, is dead."

Nanyehi and Colonel Martin carried the body of the aged chief to the council house. Nanyehi took Attakullakulla's spear and tied an eagle feather to the top and placed it outside the lodge, so that all could see that their chief was now dead and that his body awaited proper burial.

By the third day after his death, the people of the village had returned. Lame Deer, the adawehi, washed the body of Attakullakulla. He was then dressed in his best garments—his white leggings and his eagle feathers. His hair was anointed with bear's oil. His face was painted red. His body was placed on the skin of a deer.

Oconostota spoke first of his friend.

"Great and numerous are the feats of our brother, Attakullakulla. As a young warrior he earned the eagle feather in the War of Yellow River, which was fought against the Creeks. He traveled across the great water to the land of the British. There he was feasted and honored and given great gifts, which he brought back for his people. He rose to the position of White Peace Chief. His counsel has been sought by both his own people and by the white man. The Elder Spirits above will be honored that he now walks with them."

Lame Deer then lifted his voice. "O Master of Life, we commend our brother, Attakullakulla, to you. May his spirit reside in the seventh heaven."

The warriors then placed his gun, his bow, and his quiver beside their chief. As the people departed, the younger warriors lowered the body into the grave and began piling dirt atop it.

A full week did not pass before Tame Doe, mother of Nanyehi and sister to Attakullakulla, became ill. It was only three days later that she died. Nanyehi said the prayers for the departing spirit of her mother. She placed Tame Doe in a grave beside Attakullakulla. Then she returned with heavy heart to her cabin. She gave instructions to her daughter Betsy. "Tell everyone I am in mourning. I wish to be left alone. I will not see anyone or talk with anyone for seven sunrises."

On the morning of the third sunrise, however, Betsy approached her mother. "There is someone who would speak with you now. It is Thomas."

"Thomas is here?" Beloved Mother rose from her bed then and went out to speak with Thomas, servant to her husband, Bryant Ward. It had been a long time since Nanyehi had been with her husband. She was anxious to hear news from him.

After exchanging greetings, Beloved Mother invited Thomas inside. Sudi served them a warm drink made from possum grapes.

"Ghigau," began Thomas, "I have the words of my master to repeat to you. He says that he has learned of the attacks on your town. He begs you to come and stay with him. All of your family is welcome—Tame Doe, Betsy, Attakullakulla."

Nanyehi turned to her daughter Betsy.

"Betsy, you know that I cannot go, but perhaps you would. I

know that you have always been close with your father. Perhaps it would be best if you went back with Thomas."

Betsy looked at her mother anxiously. She paced back and forth across the room several times before she suddenly stopped and said, "Mother, Colonel Martin has asked me to live with him as his wife."

Nanyehi stared with open mouth at her daughter. She had been so full of grief that she had not taken notice of the looks and the conversations between her youngest daughter and this Colonel. She sat down slowly and sighed. Betsy waited for her to speak before she continued.

"And what has been your answer to Colonel Martin?"

"Mother, I would be his wife."

"Then it will be. We will inform your father of this arrangement."

Thomas stayed the night, and in the morning Beloved Mother dictated a message to Colonel Martin. The colonel wrote it down on the paper for Thomas to deliver to Bryant Ward.

Beloved Husband,

Much trouble has befallen us since I last was with you. As you have heard, we are at war with the Americans. Even our town of Chota has been invaded. My family is now safe, however.

Attakullakulla and my mother have recently died. I have promised them that I will now help Oconostota to establish peace. I fear that if my people cannot come to some agreement with your people, we will be lost as a nation.

Your daughter Betsy sends her greetings. She will soon be the wife of Colonel Joseph Martin. Perhaps you have heard of him. He has been a good friend to our family.

My daughter Catherine has recently become the wife of Ellis Harlan. He is a white trader who has also been a good friend to us. My son, Short Fellow, lives with the Chickamaugans. I have not seen him for some time. He is now a warrior of status and has acquired the name Five Killer.

I thank you for your kind offer, but I cannot leave my people at this time. I travel soon with Betsy and Colonel Martin to Long Island for the making of the peace treaty. I have been told that women do not address the white commissioners, but I am determined that I will be heard at this meeting.

I wish you well. We will visit at the first opportune time.

Nanyehi

The matter of the treaty meeting was no small matter. Colonel Campbell had sent word that if the Cherokee leaders did not send their head men to Long Island on the Holston within two moons, the army would lay further waste to the Cherokee towns.

Nanyehi and Oconostota traveled with Joseph Martin to Long Island. The white commissioner spoke first.

"We must tell you that your British allies can no longer furnish you ammunition or aid in battle. They have been overpowered in battle. The Cherokee must now look to the Americans for authority and help."

The Tassel spoke for the Cherokee. He directed his remarks to Colonel John Sevier.

"We were against this war, and we tried to restrain the young chiefs, but they would not listen. The talks I hear by your people now are quite different from what I expected. You have risen up from a warrior to a Beloved Man. I hope your speech will be good."

Colonel Sevier then spoke. "I have never had bad feelings for the Cherokee. I have always hoped to be their friends. I have fought your people in battle only to insure the safety of my own people."

Nanyehi, who was seated next to Oconostota and The Tassel, then rose and positioned herself in the center of the talking men. The white men looked at her with astonishment. They had assumed that she sat among them in the role of caretaker of Oconostota. No woman had ever spoken in the white man's council before.

Nanyehi looked out upon all gathered. She paused for a moment. When she spoke, her words rang out across the white man's council house.

"We know that women are always looked upon as nothing. But we are your mothers; you are our sons.

"Our cry is all for peace; let it continue.

"This peace must last forever. Let your women's sons be ours, our sons be yours. Let your women hear our words."

The white chiefs were much moved by these words. They took time to talk among themselves. It was decided that Colonel Christian would answer for his people.

"Mother, we have listened well to your talk; it is humane. No man can hear it without being moved by it. Such words and thoughts show the world that human nature is the same everywhere. Our women shall hear your words, and we know how they will feel and think of them. We are all descendants of the same woman. We will not quarrel with you because you are our mothers. We will not meddle with your people if they will be still and quiet at home and live in peace."

So it was that Beloved Mother's words and counsel were heard at the peace meeting.

Colonel Martin reported to her afterward: "Mother, before your speech the commissioners had planned to demand all land north of the Little Tennessee River. But your words were moving to them, and they have asked for no more new land."

Thus the treaty made on this day, the Long Island Treaty, was signed. And this was the only time, in all the time of treaty making, that new lands were not demanded of our people.

CHAPTER 18
The Time When the Children Came

Nanyehi and Oconostota were persuaded to stay the long months of winter in Long Island on the Holston River with Colonel Martin and Betsy. But when spring came, the aging Oconostota spoke. "I must return to Chota."

Colonel Martin obliged. "I will take you myself. We will travel by boat as much as possible. It will be less strenuous than by land."

Oconostota was not well on the return journey. He slept much of the time, whether he was in the boat or riding behind Nanyehi on the horse. Still, when they reached Chota, his eyes were opened and a smile spread across his face.

"It is Chota. This I know. I can tell by the smell of the river and by the feel of the wind."

Nanyehi helped him to bed that evening. But when the morning came, he would not be roused. His body was cold and stiff.

Colonel Martin then instructed his men to dig a grave. Nanyehi dressed her chief in his white leggings. She instructed the white soldiers to retrieve an old, abandoned dugout canoe, and this they used for his coffin.

There were few people who attended the burial rites of Oconostota, for there were few people living then in the village of Chota. Nanyehi asked of Hanging Maw, respected old man of the village, "Where are our people? Have they not returned from hiding in the hills? We must plant crops again this spring and prepare ourselves for the next winter."

But Hanging Maw sadly shook his head. "Many of them have gone to other towns and cities, Ghigau. They live along the Coosa River in the towns which were not destroyed. There the crops still stand, and there they may feed their families. They could not last the winter here."

Colonel Martin saw the situation. "It is not good here, Mother. Return with me to Long Island. Betsy is with child. She would do well to have her mother attend her. There is not enough here to last you through the next winter."

But Beloved Mother would not hear of such talk.

"I cannot leave Chota! I will stay, and others will hear of this, and soon they will all return, and Chota will once again be a mother town in our nation."

So Colonel Martin returned to Long Island, and Beloved Mother stayed in Chota. But when the spring rains had ended, and still no people returned to the town, a great sadness came upon her. Attakullakulla, Tame Doe, and Oconostota were no longer with her. Her daughters and her son were living on their own in places that required days of travel.

She remembered then the days of summers before, when she and her small children had spent several weeks at the home of her husband, Bryant Ward. She found herself giving instructions to Tomi to prepare their things, for they would go again to Pendleton in South Carolina.

She had always loved to visit Bryant's home. It was the place where she could relax. It was a time when she was not in charge, when no one came to her and said, "Please, help me with this," or "Can you do this for us, Ghigau?"

Bryant always treated her royally. He saw that her favorite dishes were fixed—roast venison, baked sweet potatoes, parched corn bread, and peaches in cobbler crust.

He often gave her gifts—silver and gold bracelets, colorful scarfs, and red and blue cloths for making clothes. Her favorite gift was a beautiful Appaloosa that she named "Red Sky," for she first saw him running in the field in the late afternoon when the sky was aflame in hues of red and orange.

Another treat was the bath, for Beloved Mother learned there what Bryant meant when he said the white man does not go to water, but brings the water to himself. Bryant had a lovely tub of marble. He would have one of his servants heat water, and then he would fill the tub for her and would sprinkle cologne water that smelled of rose petals. Here she could relax and allow herself to think back to the carefree days when she was Wild Rose, a young girl of the village of Chota.

As she and Tomi made the three-day ride, Nanyehi recalled these peaceful times. When they arrived, Bryant came riding out to greet them. Nanyehi could see that the last few years had aged her husband considerably. He rode in the horse-drawn cart instead of on his own horse. His hair was nearly white, but she could still see sprinkles of flashing red.

"You have finally come to your senses, Nanyehi," he said. "You will now stay with me?"

Nanyehi laughed and dismounted and ran to embrace her husband.

The days of the summer passed lazily by. Bryant walked over part of the farm every day to oversee the orchards and fields, although he walked now with the help of a cane. Nanyehi accompanied him, and they spent hours in talking of times past. They sat on the front porch in the cool of the evenings, and Bryant sang beautiful old Irish lullabies. The peaches ripened, and then the blackberries; and the days began to shorten. Nanyehi found herself sighing long sighs of contentment. She wondered if she could stay in this place forever.

But one day there came a knock on the door. It was Tomi's son, Billy.

"Ghigau, I have come to ask what is to be done with the children. There are four of them now. Mother and I have prepared their food and given them a place to sleep, but we are not sure what else to do, and we fear that more will be brought to us."

"Children? What children? There are children at my home?"

"Yes, Mother. The day after you left, a brave from Coyatee came with an infant. 'My wife has died,' he told us. 'There is no one in our village who can feed this one. I have heard that Ghigau has cow's milk.'"

"So you took the infant and fed him cow's milk?"

"We did, and he took it very well. But his father had to return to his own village and he does not have a cow, so he has left his infant with us. The next day an old grandfather from Tellico brought two small girls.

"'Their mother has died, and her husband was a British soldier who has now gone back to his motherland. My wife died also last week, and I cannot care for these two. Perhaps Ghigau will know what to do.' This is what he said. And so he left them, and then we had three children.

"Then last week, just before I left for this trip, a mother from our own village brought her son.

"'He is not really my son,' she said. 'He was my sister's. I am soon to be married and I leave for the Chickamaugan District. What if my sister returns here? Perhaps Ghigau will keep him for my sister. I would take him with me, but I fear my sister will return here for him.'

"I told them all, Ghigau, that you would be gone for a long time, and that you were a three days' ride from your home, but still they left these children."

So it was that Beloved Mother returned to Chota at the end of the summer. There she instructed Tomi and Billy to build a house for these children, and she sent word to her brother, Long Fellow, that she now needed help with this new family. She had not been home a week when a white soldier brought a child, a girl of five years, with the red skin of the Cherokee and the blue eyes of her father.

"What has happened to her parents?" asked Beloved Mother.

"Her mother died in childbirth," said the white soldier, "and her father must move on. He is afraid to live with the Indians, and he cannot bring this one to the white village."

Beloved Mother then looked at the white soldier, and she knew that it was he who was the father, but she said simply, "How kind of you to have undertaken this journey for your friend."

At this the Unaka said nothing, but looked at his boots and shifted from one foot to the other. So then Beloved Mother had five children in her care.

The people who had left Chota after the last war heard of this activity. Many of them talked among themselves and returned to live, so that there were soon families in Chota again. But never did Chota have as many people and never did it become a large town as it once was.

CHAPTER 19
The Treaty of Hopewell

The Tassel was likewise happy to see Beloved Mother when she returned to Chota, for it was he who had assumed the duties of chief. He hurried over to speak with Nanyehi.

"I send the message today to Governor Martin of Carolina. Our people from the south are unhappy. The white settlers continue to move in on our property."

He had his messenger then read the words of the message to be sent.

"Your people from Nolichucky are daily pushing us out of our lands. We have no place to hunt. Your people have built houses within one day's walk of our towns. We don't want to quarrel. We hope our elder brother will not take our land from us because he is stronger than we are. We are the first people that ever lived on this land; it is ours, and why will our elder brother take it from us? We have done nothing to offend our elder brother since the last treaty. We hope that you will take pity on us, your younger brother, and send Colonel Sevier, a good man, to have all your people moved off our land."

"It is good, what you have said, Tassel. Surely they will be moved by these words, and this situation will be taken care of."

Nanyehi and Chief Tassel were pleased to see that the government listened to the red brothers of the land, for they soon sent word to the town of Chota and the other Indian towns that they would meet with them at Hopewell, South Carolina, for the purpose of discussing their concerns.

So it was that thirty-six chiefs and nearly one thousand of our people attended this great meeting.

It was the white commissioner who spoke first.

"We are the men whom you were informed came from Congress to meet you, the head men and warriors of all the Cherokees, to give you peace and to receive you into the protection and favor of the United States, and to remove, as far as may be, all causes of future contention and quarrels. We wish that your people may be happy and know the blessings of the new change of sovereignty over this land, which you and we inherit.

"Congress is now sovereign of all our country. They want none of your lands or anything else which belongs to you. In earnest token of their regard for you, we propose to enter into a treaty which will be totally equal and fair to you.

"If you have any grievances, we will hear them and take necessary and proper action."

Chief Tassel then made his reply: "I am made of this earth. The Great Man above has placed me to possess it. What I am about to tell you, I have had in my mind for many years.

"This land we are now on is the land we were fighting for during the late contest. The Great Man made it for us to live upon. You must know, the red people are the native peoples of this land. It is but a few years since the white people have found this out. The white people are now living on it as our friends. From the beginning of the first friendship between the white and red people, beads were given as token of our friendship; and these are the beads I give to you, the commissioners of the United States, as a confirmation of our friendship."

Chief Tassel handed the commissioner the beads.

"I wish the commissioners to know everything that concerns us, as I tell nothing but the truth. They, the people of North Carolina, have taken our lands and are now making their fortunes out of them. I have informed the commissioners of the line I gave up. The people of North Carolina and Virginia have gone over it and encroached on our lands. They have gone over the line near Little River, and they have gone over Nine Mile Creek, which is but nine miles from our towns. I am glad of this opportunity to speak with the white commissioners on these matters."

Chief Tassel then took the map which was lying before the head men and marked the boundaries he spoke of.

"In the forks of French Broad and Holston are three thousand white people, living on our lands. This is a favored spot, and we cannot give it up! It is within twenty-five miles of our towns. These people must be removed!"

"These people are too numerous; they cannot be removed," replied the commissioner. "They settled there when the Cherokees were under the protection of the King of England. It is the king who should have removed them."

The Tassel then looked at Nanyehi. She could see the exasperation in his eyes.

"Is not Congress, which conquered the King of England, strong enough to remove these people?" countered the chief. The commissioners then looked towards each other, and they shifted among themselves until finally one of them spoke and assured Chief Tassel that these matters would be discussed by Congress.

The chief then made his final speech:

"We shall be satisfied if we are paid for the lands we have given up. But we will not, nor cannot, give up any more! I have no more to say—but one of our Beloved Women, who has borne and raised up warriors, would speak to you."

It was then that Beloved Mother came forward.

"I am fond of hearing that there is a peace, and I hope you have now taken us by the hand in real friendship. I look on you and the red people as my children. Your having determined on peace is most pleasing to me, for I have seen much trouble during the last war. I am old, but I hope yet to bear children who will grow up and people our nation since we are now to be under the protection of Congress and shall have no more disturbance.

"The talk I have given is from the young warriors I have raised in my town, as well as myself. They rejoice that we have peace, and we hope the chain of friendship will never be broken."

Nanyehi then placed before the commissioners two strings of wampum, a pipe, and some tobacco.

When the treaty was read, Nanyehi and Chief Tassel were pleased to hear these terms: "Any settler who fails to remove within six months from the land guaranteed to the Indians shall forfeit the protection of the United States, and the Cherokee may punish him or not as they please."

And thus the meetings were brought to a close, and the Treaty of Hopewell was signed by the red man and the white man.

CHAPTER 20
The Days of Chaos

When Nanyehi and The Tassel returned to Chota, they called a council meeting and read the words of the agreement to the people.

The Tassel spoke encouragingly: "Perhaps this is a time when we will be respected by the white man. The new government has promised us fair treatment."

But Coyote, a young brave, stood and addressed the chiefs and people.

"Near the ford of the river, within a day's walk of our town, we have seen the cabin of the Unaka settler. My brother, Red Dog, and my friend Crazed Hunter have seen another cabin just on the other side of Red Mountain."

Beloved Mother turned to Colonel Martin, Superintendent of Indian Affairs and husband to her daughter. "How can this be? Have they not been informed of the treaties?"

Colonel Martin stepped forward then and spoke.

"I am sorry. This is not such an easy matter. The settlers have informed me that their settling here is none of my business. I will have to take this matter up with my government."

Even The Tassel could not keep the bitterness from his words. "It seems that after the treaty, when boundaries are fixed and fair promises exchanged, then the white man is even faster to settle on our land. It would be well if we had no land, then we would have fewer enemies."

Now the months passed, and still the settlers were not moved, and it was clear that the white man's government would take no action. The Cherokees met again in council at Chota, and Colonel Martin was summoned to speak with them.

"We will wait no longer for talks and letters," Coyote informed Colonel Martin. "If you cannot keep your people off our land, then it is our responsibility to do so. We have heard the words of the recent treaty. The white chiefs have said, 'If any white settler fails to be moved off of Cherokee property after he has been fairly warned, then the Cherokee may punish him as they please.'"

Nanyehi then rose and addressed her brothers and sisters. "This is Chota, town of refuge. We have rebuilt our town since its destruction in the last war. We have brought the children of war unto this town that they may learn the ways of peace. Chota will be at war no more! No plans of war will be made in our council house."

The council meeting then broke up, and the people returned to their homes. The next day, Coyote and his brother and his friends were no longer in Chota. When Beloved Mother asked for them, she was told they had ridden on to Chilhowie.

On the following day The Tassel's messenger, Wind Runner, arrived with the news.

"The war party left from Chilhowie yesterday. They have slain the family of John Kirk, the white settler. His wife and ten of his children were killed. The father and the eldest son were out hunting, but all of the rest are dead."

Beloved Mother and The Tassel knew there was nothing to do but wait, for the white government would soon demand justice. It was Major Hubbard who was sent by the white council to destroy the village of Chilhowie. When this was done, The Tassel and Chief Old Abram were summoned for a peace treaty.

Beloved Mother was persuaded to stay behind this time by her daughter's husband, Colonel Martin. "Stay and visit with your daughter," he counseled his mother-in-law. "Betsy and I have been away for some time now, but you two can now be together again. I will travel with the chiefs, and we will see that this treaty is fairly made."

Privately he told Betsy, "Your mother must rest. Your people demand too much of her. The slaying of John Kirk's family and the destroying of Chilhowie is more than she can bear. Daily she counsels with herself, saying that only if she had done this or only if she had done that, then these matters might have been peacefully settled. It is too much. She will stay behind. See that she rests."

So Beloved Mother stayed behind, but she made the chiefs promise to send a messenger ahead with news.

On the day of the peace meeting, Beloved Mother gazed into the fire and shivered. "It does not go well. Something has happened."

Betsy tried to toss her mother's words aside lightly. "It is only the approaching rain which has made you feel a dark shadow. Surely things go well, and soon our chiefs will be here." But she knew her mother's thoughts and feelings to be prophetic; and she, like her mother, did not sleep well the next few evenings.

When Running Wind rode up to the cabin three days later, breathless and exhausted, the two women feared the worst.

"Ghigau," he said between gasps of air. "I have seen with my own eyes what has happened. I swear to you the truth of the events I saw."

"Running Wind, we know you to be a man of honor. Rest for a minute, and then we will listen to your story."

But Running Wind could not be quiet. He continued to talk as he panted for air. "I was with the party that rode to town with our chief men. When we entered Major Hubbard's camp, our chiefs were conducted to a cabin. They entered there, and the door was closed behind them. There was something that I did not like about the look of the Unaka soldier as he closed that door. I rode around to the back, where I could see through the window. In the cabin were several Unaka soldiers, and there were also other white men in regular clothes. I am told that one of them was the son of John Kirk. Major Hubbard handed this one a tomahawk, and the son of Kirk proceeded to kill our chiefs—all of them that were there—while the Unaka soldiers looked on!"

Beloved Mother cried out, "This cannot be! Our chiefs went under the flag of peace at the command of Major Hubbard himself. Surely not The Tassel! He has always been a man of peace!"

Beloved Mother had grabbed Running Wind's arm as she spoke. Her eyes now frantically searched his face, hoping for a denial of what she had just heard. But Running Wind looked at the ground, nodded his head, and said, "It is so, Mother."

Beloved Mother mounted her horse and rode slowly to the council house. She cried out loudly for all of the people of Chota to hear.

"Our chiefs have been killed! The Tassel and Old Abram—both have been killed! All is now out of order! Our world is in chaos! Balance and harmony cannot be restored! Nothing can be done!"

She stayed at the council square and continued to cry out, until finally she became exhausted and Tomi and Oni persuaded her to return to her own cabin. But once she was there, she would not come out, neither would she eat, neither would she talk with anyone—not even to her daughter Betsy or to her brother, Long Fellow.

Betsy then sent word to Five Killer. "You must come. Mother is no longer in her right mind. She will talk with no one. She refuses the attention of the adawehi. Come quickly."

And so Five Killer came, and after a short period she began to respond and to talk again and to resume her activities, but she would listen to no more talk of peace or war.

"Mother, they have acted as beasts, Major Hubbard and his men," Betsy began one day. Thinking her words would be of some comfort, she added, "The order has been sent for the arrest of the white soldiers who have caused this incident."

"That may be," said Five Killer, "but they will not be brought to justice by the white man, and Chief Tassel's family will not rest until his death has been avenged."

Five Killer's words proved true, for these white men were not brought to trial. So it was that vengeance was left once again to the Cherokee themselves. Doublehead and Pumpkin Boy, brothers of

The Tassel, and John Watts and Bench, nephews of the chief, led raids against the settlements.

"Doublehead has gone past the bounds of revenge," reported Five Killer one day. "He brings shame to our people."

"What has he done?" asked Betsy.

"He killed and scalped two Unaka soldiers. He and his men drank all their whiskey, and then they cut strips of flesh from the two dead men and broiled them and ate of this. Doublehead also broiled their hearts and brains."

Betsy cried out, "Tell me no more! Mother, this cannot be! Are they animals? Can nothing be done to restrain them! We cannot let this go undone. Mother, you are Ghigau. Call these men before you, and let us see that action is taken against them!" insisted Betsy.

But Beloved Mother only pointed to the fire burning in the center of the room. "The fire will eventually burn itself out, and there is nothing more to be done. We are in the midst of a great storm. It is out of control. Nothing can be done. It will wreak its destruction until its anger is completely spent. We can only wait."

"It cannot get any worse," Betsy consoled herself.

But the peace was not soon to come, and a few nights later, the entire household was awakened to the sounds of whooping men, horses, and ringing gunshots.

Five Killer and Beloved Mother rode in to Chota. There they found the people dazed and confused and crying. Mothers were holding wounded children. Children were huddled around wounded mothers. Chief Hanging Maw had his dead wife in his arms. A bullet had entered her head.

"What is the meaning of this?" Beloved Mother demanded of Five Killer.

"I am told it was a band of militiamen. They were seeking revenge for the death of a friend who was killed in a knife fight by one of our braves at the trading post."

And so the war raged on, with both sides claiming victories and demanding vengeance. In those years, Beloved Mother could do little but counsel with her friends and neighbors. She took comfort in one thing—her son, Five Killer, was also sickened by the lengths to which the warriors on both sides had gone, and so he remained for some time with her and did not return to Chickamauga.

And it was in those days that Five Killer found me near the village destroyed by the Unakas and brought me to live with Beloved Mother. So Mother passed the days attending to the needs of us children and counseling with the people remaining in the village, but she did not talk of war or peace or broken agreements.

There appeared one day a messenger from the Southern region. "Dragging Canoe is now dead, Ghigau."

Beloved Mother replied, "This I know. I have been waiting for the official word. Two nights ago I had a dream. In the dream were myself and Dragging Canoe and my first husband, Kingfisher. We were paddling down the river in a great canoe.

"How is it that this happened?" she asked of the messenger. "Was he killed in battle?"

"No, Ghigau. Things were going well. The warriors of Chickamauga had returned from raids in Cumberland and Kaintuckee, and they had many scalps. Our people were gathered at Lookout Mountain Town for dancing and celebration. The Eagle Tail Dance was performed in tribute to our great war chief, Dragging Canoe. He attended the festivities, but he retired early in the evening. He did not rise in the morning. He was dead. He simply died in his sleep."

Betsy then spoke: "Mother, Dragging Canoe has been an evil one! He is the one who has so long led the warring elements of our tribes. He is responsible for much of the bloodshed we have seen through these years. It is well that he is dead."

But Beloved Mother's words were quick and harsh to her daughter. "This is not so! I mourn the death of Dragging Canoe! We were called to different paths in life. The White Wolf called me to the path of peace, and the Great Spirit called my cousin to the path of war. He has served his people well!"

"But Mother, Dragging Canoe counseled war when you have always counseled peace!"

"Daughter," she replied, "do you not remember the days when the town of Chota was a great and powerful town? It was recognized by all as the capital of our nation. This was the time of the great chiefs Attakullakulla and Oconostota. Always the Ani-Yunwiya govern the people with two chiefs, the great white chief of peace and the great red chief of war. It is recognized that both are important to the welfare of the people, for a people must be strong and be able to look their enemies in the eye and bring fear to their faces, or else they will be pushed off of this earth. But a people must also be a peace loving people, who strive to live in harmony with themselves and those about them."

That evening Beloved Mother called a council meeting for all of the people of Chota, and she informed them of the death of Dragging Canoe. While they were gathered, she recounted for them the story of Star Woman:

"I will tell you a story that perhaps you have heard. It is a story that is not told so often any more. It was told to me by my own grandmother.

"It is said that our people spun down from Galunlati, the realm of light, through Star Woman, beloved daughter of Asga Ya Galunlati, the father of all.

"One day Star Woman heard drumming from beneath a small tree. She dug a small hole beneath the tree to investigate. When she bent over to look into the hole, she fell in. She found herself spiraling down from the Seventh Heaven to the Earth below.

"Her father was much afraid. He was not able to pull her back. So he sent winds to support her, and he inspired the creatures of earth to come to her aid. The creatures saw her spinning down upon them, and they said, 'We must do something for her; we must find a place for her to land, because she is surely a great gift.'

"Turtle said, 'She will land upon my back. I will make it strong and firm for her.'

"Some of the creatures dove into the waters in search of bits of earth to make a place for her to stand. It was Water Spider who was first successful in bringing up some earth, and this she placed upon the back of Turtle. This bit of earth grew and grew and grew. Great Buzzard came along, and he flapped his wings upon the earth, causing great ridges in the land. This is why today we have the mountains and the valleys.

"Now Star Woman fell upon Turtle's back, and there she was impregnated with fruitful winds. From her came two sons with opposite natures. The first son was born in the natural manner. His face was like that of the ascending light. The second son, whose face was like the descending night, was born from beneath his mother's arm. It was his birth which caused her death. Her decaying body brought forth grasses, grains, beans, squash, and all good things for people to eat. Her tears formed the fresh waters of our rivers.

"Brother of the Light Face worked hard and was productive. Brother of the Dark Face argued and fought against the natural order of things.

"Brother of the Light Face journeyed to find a suitable place for his people to live. Brother of the Dark Face captured the lightning, which he tended as fire burning upon the shore. There he waited for Brother of the Light Face to return from the westward journey.

"Of course, Brother of the Dark Face represents the dark side of our natures. From him come negative thoughts and actions. Yet within his action lies also the seed of good, and it is often his actions which allow the work of Brother of the Light Face, who strives to bring the light of understanding to his people.

"Thus it is throughout all time. There have always been these two forces. We cannot say that one is better than the other, but we know that they act together as a whole for the good of the people.

"Thus it has been with myself and Dragging Canoe. If it had not been for the action of Dragging Canoe, our people would now be as the Catawbas, a people who are down to only a handful because of the power of the white man."

So it was that Beloved Mother insisted that those in her household and in the village of Chota observe a time of mourning for the death of the great chief, Dragging Canoe.

When the period of mourning had ended, Beloved Mother went to the river early in the morning for the cleansing ritual. She waded out into the cold stream, dipped some water, and poured it over her head. As she lifted her face she saw, standing on the opposite bank, the white wolf. He had made his appearance for the third time in her life.

"O Brother Wolf," she called gently, "thank you for your presence."

The wolf rose and howled softly. Then he turned and went into the woods.

Beloved Mother knew then that a time of peace was to be with her people.

CHAPTER 21
The Arrival of Five Killer

The period of peace that followed was a welcome peace for both sides. Beloved Mother sent word to the White Father: "Our people would have more hoes, plows, seed, cotton carding, and looms for weaving. They would learn the way of cultivation. If you would send these things, we will put them to good use."

And this the White Father did. He also sent them agents, Benjamin Hawkins and R. J. Meigs, who were willing to come and administer and help.

And so the people of the Ani-Yunwiya learned to grow sugar and cotton and to spin thread to make cloth for clothes. Their farms were fenced, their houses were made more durable and more comfortable, and their land was stocked with cattle and hogs.

These were the days that I lived with Beloved Mother in Chota, and the days were good. We children learned both the ways of cultivation and civilization of the white man, and we learned also the stories, the legends, and the ways of being of our people, the Ani-Yunwiya.

But the problem of the land still remained. From 1804 to 1816 the Cherokee gave up large tracts of land in Georgia, Tennessee, and southern Kentucky. The town of Chota became an island more and more remote from the body of the larger settlements. It was nearly a ghost town with only a few families.

The orphan children were all grown then, and many had families of their own, and it was only I who remained with Beloved Mother. Even Long Fellow had moved from Chota and had settled along the banks of the Ocoee River.

Catherine and Betsy begged their mother to come and live with them, as did Long Fellow. But still Beloved Mother remained in Chota with a few of the old ones, and still she hoped that some day the people would return.

When word was sent that Bryant Ward was dying, Mother rushed to Pendleton to be at his side. She stayed with him in the last few days and then returned after the funeral.

When she returned to Chota, she saw for the first time the starkness of the village, and she said to me that evening, "Dancing Leaf, it is time. I have always been taught that our land was given to us by the Great Spirit. We are to be the caretakers. We hold it in trust for future generations. Our ancestors rest here. They guard and protect our land.

"But I have said my prayers to the fire each evening, and I feel that this is now the answer. We will move on."

So it was that we moved to the home of Long Fellow along the Ocoee River. We expanded his lodge and built enough rooms to house travelers. There also we had a large ferryboat so that traders and others might cross the river. We lived close to the white settlement and also close to Catherine and Betsy and their children.

But still there was the problem of the land, and sometimes there was even talk of moving west.

It was General Meigs who told the people: "The White Father in Washington will buy the rest of your land. He will give you blankets and rifles and iron pots and whiskey if you will move to the West."

The chiefs questioned the white agent: "But we have done as our White Father has asked. We have taken up the plow and the hoe and tended our crops and learned to live as the white man. And now the White Father wants us to give up our land, and he will give us rifles and whiskey if we move west and live as we once did? How can this be?

"Besides, we have heard from our brothers who have already moved west. The talk is not good from that side either. The Osage and the Quepaw Indians have laid claim to land the government has said the Cherokees could live upon. Already there is warfare there."

The Cherokee leaders met then and determined that it was time for a new way of dealing with the white government. Already too much land had been sold by chiefs who were not acting for the good of the entire nation. Thus the Cherokee Council was established with three branches of government, and it was decided that only officials of the Council could sell land or deal with the white government.

Now the Cherokee Council was to meet in the year of 1817 and discuss this matter of the white man's proposal to move west. It was to this council meeting that Beloved Mother and the other mothers of the Women's Council would send their message.

So it was that on that certain spring day Beloved Mother and I awaited the arrival of Five Killer, for he had agreed to take the message to the council meeting. And that was the day the Unaka boy came for the remedy, and the day the adawehi, Lame Deer, said the formula to drive the intruder from the bones of Beloved Mother, and the day when I first determined that I would write the story of Beloved Mother on these talking leaves.

It was past the sunset when finally Five Killer arrived. It was the sound of the dogs barking that had first alerted us. We heard then the hoofbeats of horses and the sound of voices as they tied the horses to the rail. I looked out and saw the figure of Five Killer and also another figure that I did not recognize.

And then the door was opened, and Five Killer's voice and presence filled the room.

"Ai-Ye!" he exclaimed. "Is this Dancing Leaf? I look no more at a child but at a grown woman? Can this really be?"

He lifted me up and swung me around until Beloved Mother called to him.

"Enough of this! You forget you are an old man now, Five Killer."

I looked at him and realized that it had been a long while since I had seen him and that he had aged much since then, for his hair was now gray and his body seemed not so hard and muscular. Tears came to my eyes, for it was Five Killer who was like a father to me. He had rescued me that day on the stream, and he had always brought me presents and entertained me with stories.

Five Killer saw my tears, and he joked with me, "So you have grieved in my absence. That is the way it has always been with the women in my life. Is this not so, Mother?"

"This mother would not know about the other women in your life," Beloved Mother answered him. "My hair has gone all white since your absence when you abandoned me to live with Dragging Canoe and the Chickamaugans. You have only come now and then to brag of your exploits."

Five Killer laughed loudly at this, for he knew his mother to be jesting, and he put his arms around her and drew her close, and I could see there was also a tear in her eye.

It was then that I looked around and saw the second person who was now at the door. I looked at him, and then I quickly looked away. I could see that he was a person near my own age, and suddenly I could not talk, and I wondered when was the last time I had combed my hair. I wished I had worn my blue skirt instead of the brown one.

Five Killer turned to him and said, "Come in. Meet my mother and my sister, Dancing Leaf." The young brave looked at us and nodded and then looked toward the floor.

"This is Blue Lake. He has been living with me for some time now."

I knew without asking how he had gotten this name, for although his skin and his hair were the same as the rest of our people, his eyes were the color of the blue autumn sky. They were round, and they appeared so clear that I was reminded of a beautiful lake we had seen on the way to our new settlement. He wore breeches and a blue calico shirt.

Beloved Mother said, "Dancing Leaf, do not let this handsome warrior stand in the doorway. Show him in and we will see that these two have had something to eat. They have been traveling for many hours, and I am sure their stomachs are empty."

I was glad to have something to do. I took deer stew from the pot on the fire and ladled some into each of the bowls and cut the corn bread into large pieces and gave one to each of us. In the center of the table I put the pot of sweet potatoes and a bowl of strawberries.

We were quiet as we ate, for all of us were hungry. When we finished, Blue Lake said, "I will put the horses in the shed and see to my dog who is tied outside."

Beloved Mother rose and began scraping plates. "Here," she said, "take these scraps of food for your dog."

Then she turned to me. "Dancing Leaf, get the talking paper. You will read it for these two, and we will see if they approve."

While I went to get the paper, I could hear her saying to Five Killer, "Did you know that Dancing Leaf now can read and write as good as any of the Unakas? She advanced so quickly that it is now she who teaches the younger ones."

When Blue Lake returned, I took the paper and held it near the lantern that I might better read the words. I was surprised at the sound of my voice, for the words that came from my mouth were the words of a calm person, and yet I did not feel calm at all. If it had been only Five Killer who was there I could have been proud and confident, for I knew he would be pleased and proud of my reading accomplishments. But this one, Blue Lake, was there, and I did not want to sound arrogant.

So I took care that my voice was soft and low, and not like the voice of Mrs. Gambold at the Spring Place School, whose voice rings throughout the schoolhouse and across the fields when she reads.

The Cherokee ladies have thought it their duty as mothers

to address their beloved chiefs and warriors now assembled.

Our beloved children and head men of the Cherokee nation, we address you warriors in council. We have raised all of you on the land which we now have, which God gave us to inhabit. We know that our country was once extensive, but by repeated sales has become circumscribed to a small tract. We have never thought it our duty to interfere until now. We do not wish to go to an unknown country. We have understood some of our children wish to go over the Mississippi. But this act of our children would be like destroying your mothers. Your mothers, your sisters, ask and beg of you not to part with any more of our lands, but keep it for your growing children, for it was the good will of our Creator to place us here, and you know our Father, the great President, will not allow his white children to take our country away. Only keep your hands off of paper talks! For it is our own country, for if it was not, they would not ask you to put your hands to paper, for it would be impossible to remove us all, for as soon as one child is raised we have others in our arms.

Therefore, children, do not part with any more of our land, but continue on it and enlarge your farms and cultivate and raise corn and cotton, and we, your mothers and sisters, will make clothing for you which our Father, the President, has recommended to us all.

When I had thus finished reading the words, I looked at Five Killer, but his head was bent and his eyes were toward the fire. I looked then at Blue Lake and found that his eyes were upon me, but when my eyes met his, we both looked quickly away.

"Well?" It was Beloved Mother who finally spoke. "How do you find this speech? Will it go well with the Council?"

"Yes, Mother. I am only silent for I am too moved for speech at the moment. All who hear your words will be touched by them. I hope that all will agree with you, for there are many decisions before us now."

We all knew this to be true. The decisions made in the next few months would be important ones.

"It is because of dishonest men like Doublehead that we have lost so much in the recent years," Five Killer added. "Someone should have killed that one long before it was done."

It had been some time now since the death of Doublehead. It was said that he was killed by our own head men for crimes against our people. The Unakas were glad of it anyway, for it was Doublehead who had eaten the flesh of the white men.

"How could such a one become a chief? How could he be a leader of our people?" I asked.

"He was strong, and the weaker of the tribe were attracted to his strength. The white man was afraid of him," replied Five Killer.

"But I do not understand," I continued. "How could one who so hates the white men sell our land to them?"

"Because Doublehead only really hated that which did not please or benefit him. The white man's money pleased him well, and every time he negotiated a treaty for our people, it was Doublehead who became a richer man. Doublehead was a man with livestock and granaries and stores and river crossings. He hauled his goods to the port of New Orleans in a large boat equipped with two cannons.

"How is it that he was killed?" Beloved Mother asked.

"It is said that it was ordered by the Council and that our chiefs, Ridge and Hicks and Vann, were the ones who assassinated him. Anyway, he is now gone, and we can only hope that our people will listen to wise leaders."

"What do you think of this one, Ridge?" asked Mother. "Do you judge him to be a good and strong leader? I hear often of him these days."

It was true that Ridge had risen to a position of prominence in the tribe. His children attended the mission school at Spring

Place also.

"He is a strong man. It was he who spoke against the vision of the men from Oostanaula. He is not easily swayed. He knows his mind, and he stands strong."

"Of what vision do you speak?" I asked, for I had heard of none of this talk.

Five Killer looked at Beloved Mother with eyebrows raised. I knew then that this talk had been kept from my ears.

Beloved Mother nodded, and Five Killer then answered.

"This is a story that was told to a Cherokee council meeting at Oostanaula near Rocky Mountain. It was told by three of our people who saw a vision at the same time. One was a man; the other two were women.

"They were on their way to visit a friend when the winter night descended upon them quickly. They could not make it to their friend's home, and so they found a deserted house and decided to spend the night at this place. No sooner had they entered the house than they heard a loud, crashing noise. They thought perhaps it was a terrible storm. But when they went outside, they saw a band of Indians descending from the sky mounted on black ponies. Their leaders were beating drums. A ghost rider with a drum called to them:

"'Do not fear us; we are your brothers. We have been sent by the Great Spirit. He is angry that you allow the Unakas on the land without qualifying which of them come with just cause. You can see for yourself that your hunting land is gone, and now you are planting the corn of the white people. Go and sell that corn back to them, and then you must plant Indian corn, and it will be pounded in the way of your fathers; do not use the mills of the white man. The Mother of our Nation is gone from you because her bones are being broken through the grinding.

"'There are white people among you who are corrupt and who destroy our customs and who cheat and steal from their red brothers.

Put these white people out of your world. If you do this and return to your former manner of life, then the Mother of the Nation will return to you.

"'We do not say put all of the white people out of your world. But you can see that they are entirely different beings from us. They are made of the white sand, and we are made of red clay. You may keep good relations with them, but you must get back your Beloved Towns.

"'If any of you do not believe this vision, then the Mother of the Cherokees will strike him dead.'"

At these words we all sat quietly, for they were very serious words. I looked to Beloved Mother. Her face was serious, but there was no surprise in it, and I knew that she had heard this story before. For me, it was a new story, though, and I felt as if I had just had a bad fall and the wind had been knocked from my body.

"What did the others say?" I asked of Five Killer. "Did the chiefs agree to heed these words? Are we to be at war again now?"

"There were those who judged it to be a true vision. There are many who have opposed the taking of the white man's ways. Our adawehis have long counseled us to return to the ways of our fathers. There was much talk after the testimony of these three, but it was Ridge who then rose and gave his counsel."

"What was his mind on these things?" asked Beloved Mother.

"He said that this talk would lead us again to war with the white man. He said the talk was false, that the vision was not from the Great Spirit. He said that he defied the message of the vision, that if it was indeed a true vision, then death would come upon him at that very minute.

"It was then that many of the gathered men leaped upon him and pushed him to the ground and drew their knives and would have killed him. But he fought back as a great bear, and some of our people came to his rescue. When the head chiefs demanded order, Ridge stood up and said, 'See? I still live. The vision is a deception.'"

"What do you make of the vision, Mother?" I asked.

"I do not know. I know that many of our adawehis would have us believe that we must denounce the white man's ways if we are to survive. But they are too extreme. My own vision has been the vision of the white road of peace, and it is a middle road that says that we must be adaptive and learn the good of the new ways and still respect the ways of the old. It is in this balance that we will advance as a people.

"I have listened and hearkened to my own vision, and I feel it has been a true way for me.

"But now, I do not know. I am not at peace with myself. We have gone too far and lost too much of our land. There is no one who would instruct the children in the old ways. No one tells them the stories. We do not celebrate the seven festivals as we once did. Only the Green Corn Festival is still celebrated by a few. This is not good. We must take care to preserve the ways of our people!"

Five Killer and I looked at each other then, for Mother's voice had begun in her usual soft and restrained way of speaking, but by the time she had finished, her voice was shrill and her words quavered and her hands rose and trembled.

Five Killer said, "We do not need to leave in the morning. We will stay another day. It is good that we visit and counsel with you. It would be good if we stayed another day."

I sighed a breath of relief and helped Mother to her bed. I showed Five Killer and Blue Lake to their room, and then I also retired for the evening.

But sleep did not come quickly. The fire continued to crackle, and a coyote howled in the distance. I wondered if there were coyotes in the land on the other side of the Mississippi. I wondered if the land there was a land of mountains.

I thought of Blue Lake. Where had this one come from? Who were his parents? It would have been rude to have asked, but tomorrow I hoped to learn these things.

Finally I drifted to sleep. That night I dreamed of swimming in a clear, blue lake.

CHAPTER 22
The Day after Five Killer Came

I arose before the others in the morning. Quietly I made my way through the cabin in the gray of the early morning. Outside, the air was cool, and I shivered for a moment and watched my breath as it formed small puffs of steam. The sky was clear, and I could see the long fingers of the sun stretching up over the hills to the east. I judged that it would be a clear, dry day. That would be good. I hoped the spring rains were now behind us. The ground was still soft, but with one more day of dry weather, Billy could begin the planting.

I made my way along the stone path to the shed where the animals were kept. Billy was already there, milking our brown and white cow. She was a skinny cow, but she gave good milk. It was thick and sweet. The black cow that we had had before was much heavier, but her milk was thin and bluish.

Billy handed me the bucket. He would fill one more for his family.

"Who is the one with the blue eyes?" he asked.

"I only know he is called Blue Lake."

"Well, he looks to be about your age. What do you think of him? Is there a reason Five Killer brought him along?"

"I have too many other things to think about. I do not know about this." My answer was short.

I crossed the shed to the other side, where the black and white speckled hens were clucking. The hens were gifts from the Unakas. Caroline Young had given them to Mother after the birth of her last son. Mother had been there to help.

When I returned, I saw that the others had now also risen and were already being served breakfast. Sudi had prepared the hominy mush, and she was ladling some into each of the bowls. Strips of dried deer meat were lying on a plate in the center of the table. A bowl of dried peaches was also before us.

I knew that Five Killer would not drink milk, but I scooped a cup from the pail and offered it to Blue Lake. He nodded his agreement, and I set it before him. I scooped one for myself then and sat down.

Long Fellow and Five Killer had already begun eating and were nearly half finished. But this one, Blue Lake, had not touched anything on his plate yet. Perhaps he had spent time living with the Unakas, for his manners were more like those of the white settlers. I knew that he would use the fork and spoon before him, for I had seen him use them the night before. Long Fellow and Five Killer still used their fingers.

Mother said to me, "Long Fellow, Five Killer, and myself will ride out today. We will spend some time in the settlement visiting with Lame Deer and Hanging Maw and the others. We will be back in the late afternoon."

She paused for a minute, then she added, "Blue Lake can stay here with you. Show him all the things around here. Perhaps you two can catch a fish for supper."

At these words I dropped my fork, and it made a loud clang on my plate. Everyone looked at me.

Blue Lake stood and said to Mother, "I thank you. I will go now and feed my dog."

Beloved Mother rose to fix a bowl of scraps for the dog. When Blue Lake had gone outside, I turned to Mother. "I do not even know this one. You would leave him with me for a full day? Of what will we talk?"

"Five Killer tells me he attends the mission school at Brainerd. You will find much to talk about."

Mother arose as if the matter were thus decided.

Blue Lake and I stood on the porch and looked out as they drove off in the horse-drawn wagon. Their figures bounced unevenly as the old wagon made its way along the rutted road. This would not be good for Beloved Mother. Surely her joints would be in pain again. But perhaps not—perhaps the adawehi had come at just the right time, and perhaps his sacred prayers had taken effect.

I looked down when I felt a tugging at my foot. It was Blue Lake's dog pulling on my moccasin strings. He was a handsome dog, about the size of a wolf, only thicker in build.

"What is his name?" I asked.

"It is a she. I call her Chera."

Her fur was reddish-orange with black tips on the end. Chera was a good name for her, for Chera means fire.

Blue Lake grasped her jaws and scolded her for playing with my shoe.

"I like her," I said to him. "How old is she?"

"She is only nine moons. She is still a pup. But already she is a good watchdog, and I will train her for the hunt."

I reached over and massaged the area behind her ear. She rolled her head in pleasure.

"You do not have a dog of your own?" he asked.

"I did once. A big black dog. I called her Star. But she was bit by the rattlesnake, and Long Fellow had to shoot her."

"Oh." We were both silent for a moment.

"We could ride over to the mounds," I suggested. "From there you can see many things."

"You do not need to worry with me," he said. "I can amuse myself. I could see the look you gave your mother this morning. Perhaps I will take Chera for a hunt."

I looked at him then, but he was looking out to the sky. I could not judge his words, so I turned and went into the house and put on my riding skirt.

When I came out, he was still sitting there. I went to the barn and put the rope around the necks of Smokey and Red Sky and fitted the wooden pieces into their mouths. I led them out to the front of the porch and stood facing Blue Lake.

"You can ride Smokey," I said. "I will ride Red Sky."

We both mounted, and Blue Lake whistled for Chera to follow.

"The mounds in the distance," I began, "were the burial grounds of a tribal people that lived before us on this very land."

We rode in silence for a while, and then Blue Lake said, "You read very well. How did you learn?"

"I go to Spring Place," I answered. "But I have come home for the planting season. I don't know if I will return in the fall."

"How old is your mother?" I knew then that he understood my reason for not wanting to return.

"I judge her to be close to eighty years. Five Killer himself is close to sixty years."

We said nothing for a while, and then I said, "I am told you go to the Brainerd Mission."

"I did. I go no more."

"Tell me of that place. I have heard much of it."

"It is a good enough place. They have a large house with one floor stacked on top of another. We sleep on the top floor and live and eat and have school and services on the bottom floor."

"How did you spend the days there?"

"The boys got up early and took turns at morning chores—feeding the animals, milking the cows, cutting the wood. When the horn was blown, we would gather for the morning prayer service. Bible verses were read. Then we did our lessons of grammar and arithmetic and practiced our writing. In the afternoon we worked in the fields. On Sundays we were not allowed to do anything, for the white man's Bible says that it is to be a day of rest."

"So you can read and write also?"

"Yes, but I learned that in a school back in Virginia."

"You have lived in the East?"

"Not for very long. My father was a trader, and he wanted me to learn the white man's way. He had a white family in Virginia. But my mother was a full-blood, and she wanted me to live the way of the Indian. So Father took me one day and said we were going on a hunting trip, but we never returned to my mother's house, and we went all the way to Virginia."

"What did you do there?"

"I cried and I wouldn't eat, and I became so thin that the white doctor told my father I couldn't adjust, and so I was sent back to my people. But when I got there, Mother had died. I lived with my grandfather until he died, and then I was sent to Brainerd."

"But now you will not return there?"

"There are things I didn't like about it. I ran away one day to Chickamauga, and that is where I met Five Killer and it was agreed that I could stay with him."

We rode on past the wooded area and came out to the meadow in front of the mounds. The mist of the morning had cleared, and the sky was blue with great white puffs of clouds. He asked me then, "How is it with Spring Place?"

"It is well enough. I like Brother and Sister Gambold. They are kind to us. We do the same things you talk about, and I now help the younger ones with the learning and reading."

I pointed ahead to the lone tree to the right of the first mound. "I will race you to that tree," I said. I gave Red Sky a kick and was off before he could answer me.

He soon passed me, though, and when I got to the tree, he had already dismounted and was sitting.

"You see that I have given you the faster horse," I said.

"Yes, I see that," he said as he smiled.

I noticed then the whiteness of his teeth and how straight and even they were. His eyes matched the blue of his shirt and the blue of the sky that day. I would have told him how much I liked the color of his eyes, but it did not seem the right thing to say. Nor did I sit next to him, as I would have liked to, but I sat a little distance from him.

"Why did you leave Brainerd?" I asked.

"I became angry one day. They forced the children to memorize and recite Bible passages when they were judged to have done something wrong. They scared the small ones with the talk of the everlasting burning fire. They told them they would burn in this fire forever if they did not behave and do as their commandments say.

"So one day I stood up and said loudly that I did not believe that such a fire existed and that our children were not to be scared by these things any more. After that I left."

"I do not believe in that fire either," I added.

We both sat quietly and watched as the wind blew waves into the grass of the meadow.

Then I said, "Do you believe the vision of the people of Oostanaula? Do you think it to be a message from the Great Spirit?"

"I do not know," he answered. "I would not argue with another man's vision, for I have had visions of my own. So I do not know. What do you think?"

"I do not know either. It is the first time I have heard such talk, although the adawehis are always warning us to return to the teachings of the old way, that we will be destroyed if we do not. But then the teachers at the mission tell us we would burn in the everlasting fire if we do not accept their ways. It is not easy to know what to do these days."

I reached up and tickled Chera on her belly, for she had stretched out on her back with her feet in the air.

"This is a long way for her. She is exhausted," I said.

Blue Lake stood up and stretched and looked about. He said to me, "I will race you on foot to the top of that first mound. I will not begin running until you have reached the bottom of the mound."

I jumped up and was off without answering him. When I reached the bottom of the mound, I looked back to see that he was removing his moccasins. I wished I had thought to do likewise, for he would be able to better grip the side of the mound as he went up with his bare feet.

I knew I could not look back again, and I began the ascent, trying to watch my footing and leaning my body forward for better balance.

When I had judged myself to be three quarters of the way up, I heard his breath nearly upon me, and then he passed me. I tried to speed up, but then I felt something nipping at my heels. It was Chera. Finally, I hoisted myself over the top to the flat place on top with Chera still attached to my heels. Blue Lake was there with his arms folded in front of his chest. He was looking down at us. And then I started laughing and could not stop, and Chera was then in my face, licking me. It felt good to laugh, for I had not done so for a long time, not since the time Mother and I found a raccoon with Long Fellow's moccasin.

Blue Lake was then pulling Chera from me and smiling broadly himself.

"So now you put your dog upon me so that I might lose. If you had not done so, surely I would have won."

"Surely you would have," he answered as he extended his hand to help pull me up.

The wind blew hard on the top of the mound, and my hair was whipped about my face. Blue Lake reached and took my hair in his hands. He held it for a minute and then arranged it behind my back. I was very close to his face. I tripped forward, perhaps it was a little on purpose, for then I was in his arms. We looked into each other's eyes, but then we both quickly took a step backward.

"See our farm?" I pointed to it. "I like the way it looks from up here. The fences are all straight. In the summer you can see the rows of planted corn."

I pointed out the Unaka settlement to the west and the flour mill on the Ocoee River to the north of us.

"Spring Place is only a little ways past Red Mountain there to the east," I said.

As I turned back to Blue Lake, I could see that his hands shaded his eyes, and he stared intently to the south.

"Are you expecting visitors?" he asked. "Two men are riding toward the lodge."

"No. But the traders are always coming. It is nothing to worry about."

"I think we should go back now. We should not leave the place unattended."

We descended the mound, walking in a sideways fashion to keep from rolling. Chera started out too fast, and she went into a roll with feet over head, until she stopped at the bottom and came up surprised at what had just happened to her.

We rode back quickly to the cabin and said very little on the way. I noted the two horses tied to the front post. One was a red roan. I knew I had seen it before. When I heard the laughter from the porch, I recognized the sound and knew who it was.

"It's Whiskey Joe," I said in a loud whisper.

"So you know him?"

"Mother does not like him. She has spoken to the white agents about him. The last time he was here, he stayed and drank all day and shot at our animals and made rude remarks to us."

We took the horses to the barn. Billy was there.

"He's drunk." Billy said, "And his friend probably is too. I would not go near the house if I were you. I'll water the horses, then maybe you two should ride out for help."

"I cannot leave," I said. "This one is a thief. I will talk with him. He is only drunk. We will give him something to eat, and then he will leave."

We returned to the cabin and found Whiskey Joe inside. He had his foot and his whiskey bottle propped on the table. His friend sat across from him.

"Well, look who it is!" he exclaimed. "It's little Dancing Leaf, and she's all growed up now! You always was a pretty thing, and you're looking even better now. Who's your half-breed friend here? What have you two been doing up there in them woods?"

"Mother is not here," I informed him. "Perhaps you should have something to eat and then be on your way."

"Where's Long Fellow?"

"He is with her also." I knew when I saw Blue Lake's face that I had said the wrong thing, so I added, "They will return soon, though, and Five Killer is with them."

"Well truth is, Dancing Leaf, we just saw them headed to the village, and hell, it would take them a full day to get there and visit and come back. I judge they won't be home for a while. What do you say, Tommy?"

Tommy nodded and grinned and looked at me with eyes going up and down. His face was dirty, and he was missing one front tooth. I thought him to be the ugliest man I had ever seen.

Whiskey Joe then said, "I think little Tommy here kinda likes you, Dancing Leaf. I do, too, you know. Why don't you just entertain us with one of them Injun dances, huh? I'd like to see how you got that name—Dancing Leaf. You must be one good dancer. Twirl that skirt around some, and let us see your legs. It's been a while since I saw a girl's legs. Hell, it's been too long since I had me a woman. I might just have one today!"

Blue Lake took a step forward then and said to Whiskey Joe, "I think you and that one should leave. I think you should leave now!"

But Whiskey Joe withdrew a gun from under his belly where it had been stuck in his belt.

"I don't take orders from no Injun," he said. "Especially not no half-breed!"

He motioned to Tommy. "Go on out to my horse. I got a rope in the right saddlebag. We'll tie him up. I don't think he'll stay shut up till we do."

He pointed the gun at me.

"You!" he said. "You sit down there for a minute. Sit right there where I can watch you."

I looked at Blue Lake. My heart was pounding so loudly that I was sure that he could hear it. But his face was calm. His eyes followed Tommy as he went out the door. I thought to cry out for Billy, but I knew he had no gun. He would not come to the cabin. I could see no way to avoid what I feared would happen.

But then the matter was quickly decided, for as soon as Tommy had exited and we heard his boots clomping down the steps, Blue Lake moved forward, and with one swift motion he kicked the chair from underneath Whiskey Joe. The bullet went from the gun with a loud noise. I looked up and saw the hole in the ceiling. Blue Lake then had the gun in his hand and was pointing it at Whiskey Joe.

"Move!" he shouted to me. "Move away from him!"

I regained my senses and did as instructed. Blue Lake backed toward the door, but he held the gun pointed at Whiskey Joe, and he said, "Don't you move anywhere! You stay right where you are."

He opened the door carefully and shouted to Tommy, "I have the gun now. Throw that rope on the ground, and you had better get out of here and get out of here fast."

We heard the hoofbeats of his horse as he rode off.

I ran out and quickly picked up the rope. When I came back in, I held the gun while Blue Lake wound the rope around and around the chair and Whiskey Joe, and then he tied a knot. He cut the rope, and with the remaining piece he tied Whiskey Joe's feet.

Whiskey Joe was hollering and threatening the whole time, so that when he had finished tying him, Blue Lake stuffed a piece of cloth in his mouth.

I went out to the barn to inform Billy of the happenings and to instruct him to ride to the Unaka settlement and to see what could be done with this one. Then I returned to the cabin.

The hours of the afternoon then stretched out before us, and we wondered what we should do until the others returned. The Unaka was soon asleep, and his head rolled forward. We could hear him snoring even through the cloth stuck in his mouth.

"The whiskey will now take effect," said Blue Lake, "and he will be out for a long time."

Blue Lake and I talked and told stories of our people. I showed him my books and my writing.

"You do not remember anything of your parents and the village before?" he asked.

I shook my head. "I do not want to."

As the sun disappeared over the side of the mountain, we heard the sound of the wagon and the horse. Long Fellow exclaimed as he lighted from the wagon, "That's Whiskey Joe's horse!"

They all burst in upon us then and stood with rounded mouths as they saw Whiskey Joe tied in the chair and Blue Lake with the gun.

Soon after that, Jeremiah Young from the Unaka settlement came riding in with two soldiers.

"We thank you, Blue Lake," the tall one said. "Whiskey Joe is wanted for murder by our people. They say he killed old man Parson from Turkey Creek in a fight over horse thieving. Seems he's just been traveling further and further down the bad road, and now there's no turning back. He'll be hung. I'm sure of it."

That night after dinner, Mother brought from her sacred box her peace pipe and some tobacco. She said her prayers to the fire and burned the tobacco in the pipe so that the prayers might be carried with the smoke to the spirit world above. Her prayers were for the safe passage of Five Killer and Blue Lake and for the success of the council meeting.

We sat and talked for some time, and then we all went to bed.

I listened to Mother as she tossed and turned. Several times she moaned and cried out. It had been too much for her, I judged. The long day. The riding out to the village. The visiting and the return. The sight of Whiskey Joe.

I crept over to her and knelt beside her.

"What is it, Mother? I fear you are having a bad dream."

She sat straight up then and looked past me as if I were not there.

"I have seen it!" she exclaimed in a loud whisper. "A great line of our people. Marching on foot. Mothers with babies in their arms. Fathers with small children on their backs. Grandmothers and grandfathers with large bundles. They were marching west, and the Unaka soldiers were behind them. They left behind a trail of corpses—the weak and sick who could not survive the journey."

She moaned softly and began rocking back and forth, holding her knees in her arms and chanting words I did not recognize.

"It is all right," I said as I sat behind her and put my arms around her. I cradled her body in mine and rocked back and forth.

"It was only a bad dream." I assured her. I rocked with her until she had quieted and I judged that she was asleep.

I unwound myself then and laid her gently down and slept close to her for the rest of that night.

CHAPTER 23
The Time We Awaited the News
of the Council Meeting

The next morning I awoke with Chera sniffing at my face. I sat up quickly, for already I judged that it was late. I could see the sun through the crack in the ceiling. I could see the form of someone at the doorway, and when my eyes had adjusted, I could see that it was Five Killer.

"You two would sleep all day and leave us to depart on our own," he scolded.

Mother and I then quickly arose and made our way to the outer room. Sudi was already there, filling the bowls with hominy mush. Five Killer was coming in and out, putting things in his pack. Long Fellow sat already at the table. I looked around, and Long Fellow said, "Blue Lake is readying the horses."

I scooped a bowl of mush for myself and one for Mother. Five Killer sat down with us, and we all ate quietly.

"You have the message on the paper?" Mother asked of Five Killer.

"I have the message, Mother. It will be delivered."

Mother then went into her room and returned with a pouch. "It is the medicine pouch of your father. I myself have put the root of campion in it, so that you may not fear the snakebite on your journey. I have kept your father's pouch all these years, but it is right that you have it now."

Five Killer took the pouch and wound the attached string around his neck.

I went into my room and took a rock from under the corner of my sleeping mat. It was an orange and white rock with streaks of clear crystal. I took a leather thong and tied it securely around this rock, and then I went outside.

Blue Lake was there with Chera. He had taken a rope and tied it around her neck, and he was tying the other end to the post of the porch.

"What are you doing with Chera?" I asked.

"This one is still too young for such a trip, but now she is too big to ride on the horse in front of me. I would leave her here, if that goes well with you. I will return for her when she is older."

I bent down and and put my arms around Chera and rubbed the favorite place behind her ears. She licked my face.

"I will keep her well," I said. "I will teach her some manners also."

I stood up then and opened my hand with the rock.

"I have had this rock for a long time. I picked it up from the banks of the river on the day that Five Killer found me years ago, and I have kept it all this time as the only remembrance of my first life.

"I would give it to you now in appreciation of what you did for me yesterday. I do not know what would have happened to me if you had not been there."

Blue Lake took it from my hand and gazed at it for a moment, then he put the leather string around his neck. He smiled at me and said, "Thank you, Dancing Leaf."

I breathed a sigh of relief then, for if he had simply put it in his pocket, I would have known it meant nothing to him.

Beloved Mother and Long Fellow and I stood on the porch as Blue Lake and Five Killer mounted their horses. We called a final farewell as they rode away. Chera ran out as if to follow them, but she was jerked back when she came to the end of the rope. She yelped and whimpered and looked at me and then back out to Blue Lake in the distance. I went to her and knelt down and put my arms around her.

"Do not worry, Chera," I said. "He will be back for you." And I thought to myself, "Perhaps he will be back for me, also."

We watched until they had approached the wooded part, and then they turned and waved at us one last time. We lifted our hands in return. They entered the woods then, and we saw them no longer.

Beloved Mother and Long Fellow and I sat on the front porch for a long while and said nothing.

Finally Mother spoke. "Let us hitch the horse to the wagon and ride out over the land today."

We went first to see the fields. "I think we will have more rows of corn this year." Mother declared. "And I would have more pumpkin and squash for the fall. Do you think," she asked Long Fellow, "that a fence would keep the raccoons and rabbits from the garden?"

Long Fellow shook his head. "No, but this one will," he said as he pointed to Chera, "She will be a good watchdog for us."

We rode around to the other side of the farm, where there was a steep hill with a lone shady tree. We got out of the wagon there and climbed to the top. The valley stretched out below us.

"Here I will be buried," Beloved Mother said.

Long Fellow answered, "It is a good spot. I would be here, too."

We rode back down into the valley and stopped at the ford of the river which ran along the back of our lodge.

"The water is still high," Long Fellow said. "It will be two more weeks of dry weather before it is at normal level."

We returned to the cabin when the sun was directly above us. Long Fellow and Beloved Mother would rest for the afternoon, until the time of the evening meal. While they slept, I took out my pen and paper, and it was on this day that I began to record the stories of Beloved Mother—the stories of her life and of our people, the Ani-Yunwiya.

After I had worked some, and my back and arms were tired from sitting in such a position, I called to Chera and we went to the river.

I took my fishing basket with me. I rolled large rocks and made a small dam so that the water pooled in one area, and then I waited until a large brim fish had entered there. Chera barked and charged at the water excitedly at the sight of the fish, but I called to her to hush. I scooped the fish from the water and then showed it to Chera, who sniffed and barked and then jumped back when the fish flopped and splashed droplets of water upon her.

By the time I got back, Sudi was there, and she set about to clean the fish and fix it for our supper.

We passed the days in this way. When the planting time was over, I still did not return to the school at Spring Place. The corn was then knee-high, and we had rows of beans and squash. I could also see the pumpkins, which would continue to grow until the harvest time. And I continued to write every afternoon while Beloved Mother and Long Fellow napped.

One day, late in the afternoon, the agent from the government came and spoke with Mother.

"Nancy," he said, "it is stated in our last treaty with your people that any Cherokee family has the right to receive a reservation of six hundred and forty acres. You only have to report to the government office and declare yourself to be a citizen of the United States."

The next day Mother announced, "We will ride into town. We will register for our reservation."

"Hmphh!" Long Fellow began. "The Unakas should be coming to us, and we would then decide whether or not they may stay on the land they have already settled."

"Yes," Mother agreed. "That is how it should be. But they are more powerful, and so we must live by their laws."

We rode to the Unaka settlement then, and Mother registered her name in the book there. The land agreement was read to us, and a copy was given to Mother.

When we returned home, Mother asked that I read the words to her again. The paper gave the boundaries of our land: "…the section of land one mile below John McIntosh's on Mouse Creek where the Old Trace crosses said creek leading from Tellico Block House to Hiwassee Garrison. Beginning at the ford and running down said creek for a compliment conformably to a treaty between the United States and the Cherokee Nation concluded on the 8th day of July 1817."

Mother was pleased to have this paper. She said to Long Fellow, "It is good to have our claim on the white man's paper."

It was that afternoon that Black Fox from Tellico rode to our house with a message from Five Killer.

"The council meeting has concluded," he informed us. "Five Killer travels to Chickamauga first, and then he will return to this place. He has decided to abandon his land there and to take up residence here and to register for a reservation just to the west of your land."

Beloved Mother and I then looked at each other. We smiled broadly, for we were pleased at such talk.

"How goes it with the council meeting?" Beloved Mother asked.

"The talks were good. Governor McMinn proposed a sale of the Cherokee land for $100,000. He said that his soldiers could no longer protect our lands and that we would best be advised to move to the western paradise beyond the Mississippi. But the chiefs and people gathered had heard the words of you, Ghigau, and of the other mothers of the Women's Council, and all were in agreement. When the vote was taken, every one of the chiefs voted 'No'!"

Beloved Mother and I then clapped our hands and broke into laughter, and we put our arms around each other.

"When will Five Killer be here?" asked Beloved Mother.

"He judges that it will be soon, before the time of the Green Corn Festival."

Beloved Mother then said, "Come inside, Black Fox. We will fix you something to eat, and you will stay and talk a while with us this afternoon."

"That would be good," answered Black Fox. "I will just see that my horse is fed and watered first and put out of the hot afternoon sun."

"I will help you," I said, and I took his horse by the reins, and we headed toward the barn.

On the way, I said to Black Fox, "Do you know of the one named Blue Lake? He is the young one who travels with Five Killer. The one with the blue eyes. Have you seen him? Will he also arrive with Five Killer?"

I hoped that my words did not sound too anxious.

Black Fox looked at me and smiled. "Oh, Dancing Leaf, I had nearly forgotten. I have something for you. It is a message from this one, Blue Lake. He has recorded his words on paper. It is a good thing you ask, for I had nearly forgotten it."

His eyes twinkled as he talked, and I could see that his mouth was turned up at the corners.

I stopped then and handed the reins to Black Fox. While he walked on toward the barn, I opened the folded paper and saw there the neatly arranged words from Blue Lake.

Dancing Leaf,

    I will arrive with Five Killer at the time of the Green Corn Festival. I have worn the stone you gave me around my neck every day since we left.

    How is it with Chera? Has she learned manners? I look forward to seeing both you and her.

    The council meeting has gone well. The chiefs and people gathered were much moved by the word of the Women's Council.

    I will see you soon.

Blue Lake

I folded the paper and took it into the house. I put this paper with my own writings in a box covered with deerskin. That is where I have kept all of my most treasured things.

CHAPTER 24
The Dancing of the Leaves

It was soon the time of the Green Corn Festival. Beloved Mother and Sudi and I swept the cabin well. We removed the old broken pottery and baskets. Billy and Long Fellow mended the walls of our cabin and tended to the outer buildings.

The chiefs were in the fourth day of fasting. The formal celebration would begin in three more days. Red Dog, from nearby Coyatee, arrived in the early morning, informing us that Five Killer would arrive later in the day.

The day passed in a lazy fashion. Mother and I rode out in the wagon and gathered blackberries from the bushes that grew along the old warpath. We then gathered nuts and acorns from the wooded area. The sky was clear blue, and as we looked across the meadow, we could see that already some of the leaves were beginning to turn colors of red and yellow. A cool breeze blew across the meadow. I watched as the butterflies flitted from one flower to the next along the side of the rutted road.

In the afternoon, Beloved Mother took a nap, and I continued to work on my writing. When Mother arose from her nap, she sat in her rocking chair on the front porch. As the sun descended in the sky, I took a blanket to her and wrapped it about her.

"The air is cool now in the evenings," I said. "Perhaps it would be better to wait for Five Killer inside."

"No," she replied. "I prefer to sit here. The blanket will keep me warm."

So I went back inside and continued with my writing, but I arose and glanced out at her from time to time. She soon dozed off to sleep with her head resting forward on her chest.

I thought to call out to her and say, "You are only sleeping. You cannot see anything coming anyway." But I knew that she would just scold me.

"I am not sleeping!" she would insist. "I am only resting my eyes from the slanting rays of the sun."

When the sun was no longer visible, and only the red and purple clouds lingered behind, I went out to the porch, and gently I placed my hand upon her shoulder.

"Mother, you would do well to come in now. It is getting too cool, and Five Killer will not care if you wait for him inside."

But she said nothing in return, and when I shook her gently, her body fell forward. Quickly I reached to catch her. I leaned her head back on the chair, but still she was not roused from her sleep. Again I shook her, and I said, "Mother, what is wrong? Wake up now and we will go inside."

Her body felt stiff. I put my ear to her lips, but I did not feel any breath. I put my ear to her chest, but I did not hear the beating of her heart. I ran inside and called loudly to Long Fellow. Then I ran out to the yard and called to Sudi and Billy. I ran back onto the porch and took Beloved Mother in my arms and shook her again. "Mother, please wake up! Please wake up!"

The others were soon there when they heard my cries. Long Fellow lifted her face back from my shoulder and listened also for her breath. He shook his head sadly and said to me, "She is no longer with us, Dancing Leaf. Her soul is now passing to the higher places."

But I shook my head fiercely and stomped my foot on the ground. I insisted that I sit there with her and rock her in my arms until Five Killer arrived.

It was dark when I first heard the horses of Five Killer and Blue Lake. Chera barked and charged outside, but I heard her threats turn to whimpers of delight when she saw who had come.

Long Fellow was there quickly with a lantern. He went out to the hitching post, and I could hear the sound of low voices.

The three of them—Long Fellow, Five Killer, and Blue Lake—then came forward and mounted the stairs. I looked up at them, and still I was rocking gently with Beloved Mother in my arms.

Five Killer came forward, and he took Beloved Mother from me and held her in his arms himself and cried softly. Then he said to me, "She is gone from this world now, Dancing Leaf. You must accept that. Let us take her into the house and lay her on her bed. We cannot sit out here with her."

He lifted her body and headed toward the door. Blue Lake was then behind me; and when I turned, his arms were around me and I cried and buried my head in his shoulder. We stood thus for a long time on the porch.

Sudi prepared a dinner for us, but no one would eat much. I returned to the porch, wrapped a blanket around myself, and looked at the stars. I wondered just exactly where the upper worlds were and if Beloved Mother was there with the people that had gone before her—Tame Doe and Attakullakulla and Dragging Canoe and all of the others.

The next morning, even before the sun appeared, Billy rode out to inform the people in the nearby settlements of Beloved Mother's death.

By late afternoon Betsy and Colonel Martin had arrived with their children and even children of their children. Catherine and Ellis Harlan also arrived with their family.

It was determined that the burial service would be held in the council house near the office of the Cherokee agent. The ceremony was attended by many of the Ani-Yunwiya and many of the Unakas. The adawehi, Lame Deer, said the proper petitions that Beloved Mother would be released from this place, that her soul might soar to the upper worlds and dwell there in the white house of happiness. The minister from the mission school said the prayer of the Great Shepherd.

When the talks were finished, the women of the village sang the song of the departing spirit. And while they sang, there arose from the body of Beloved Mother a white light. All of us there saw it. And it arose and seemed to be at one time in the shape of a white wolf, and then it appeared to take the shape of a white swan. It fluttered about and then departed through the window and flew off in the direction of the beloved town of Chota.

The people turned to each other and said, "Did you see it?"

And many went outside to see if the white light could still be seen, but it was no longer visible.

We all went in a procession of wagons to the grave site. We left the wagons at the bottom, and we got out and walked to the top, where the grave already had been dug. Five Killer and Colonel Martin and several young braves carried the coffin. It was then lowered into the ground. The women of the Ani-Yunwiya placed iron pots, clay pots, baskets, and cooking utensils into the grave with Mother. Dirt was thrown on top until all was covered. Each of us then looked for a rock, and these we placed around the grave.

The others left and proceeded back to the cabin, but Blue Lake and Chera and I remained for some time, until Blue Lake said to me, "Dancing Leaf, I feel drops of rain, and the wind has started to blow from the west. I fear a storm is upon us."

So we walked down the hillside and mounted the wagon and returned to the cabin.

In the next few weeks I felt that a gray cloud surrounded me. I spoke very little; I ate very little. I did nothing but sit on the front porch in the rocking chair. Blue Lake took me each afternoon to the grave on top of the hill, and I stayed there with Chera until the time of the setting sun.

The others said to me, "You have mourned long enough, Dancing Leaf. Beloved Mother would not have it this way. She has gone on to a better place, and she watches you with sadness from where she is. She would that you be happy."

But still, I could not help myself, and my mind and my feelings were a great blank, and nothing seemed to matter.

But I looked out one day and saw that it was again the time of changing seasons. The sky was clear blue with great puffs of white clouds. The leaves upon the trees were clothed in their best attire— red and yellow and shades of fire color. Blue Lake said to me on that day, "I will wait for you here today, at the bottom of the hill. You do not need to stay all afternoon."

I said nothing and went to the top again with Chera. When I got there, I looked out and saw our farm below and the shadows of the mountains in the distance. I heard the rustle of the leaves in the trees overhead. I looked up at the leaves, and they seemed to be dancing about. Several of them dropped from the tree and skipped across the top of the hill. Chera barked and ran in circles chasing them. I laughed when I saw this.

It felt good to laugh again. I turned when I heard someone laughing with me. There in the sky, next to the tree, was the form of Beloved Mother. She looked as she had that day long ago when we children were gathering nuts and berries. She was raising her arms and turning in small twirling circles.

She called out to me, "Daughter, in this life, do not forget the importance of this one thing—do not forget to dance!" And I was laughing and dancing then also. And Chera was barking and chasing after me. Blue Lake called out from below. I motioned for him to come up. When he had ascended the hill, he said to me, "Dancing Leaf, what is it that you do?"

"I am dancing, Blue Lake. Chera and I are dancing with the leaves. Come and dance with us."

Epilogue

The dream of Nancy Ward, Beloved Woman of the Cherokee, proved to be prophetic.

Although the Cherokees continued to make giant strides in their advancement and acceptance of the white man's "civilization," the state governments of Tennessee and Georgia brought increasing pressure on the national government to remove the Cherokees from their boundaries and to relocate them to the West.

On December 29, 1835, thirteen years after the death of Nancy Ward, a removal treaty was signed. In May 1836 President Jackson proclaimed that the treaty was binding on all Cherokees and called for the removal process to begin. From 1836 to 1838 two thousand Cherokees journeyed west. They suffered greatly during this time. Many died from cholera, pellagra, and other diseases.

In 1838, when it became clear that the majority of the Cherokees would not abandon their homes willingly, the United States government took action to see that they were forcibly removed. The remaining Cherokees were dragged from their homes and put in stockades. They were forced to march westward, leaving behind most of their supplies and possessions. Many of the three thousand captive Indians died of disease, exposure, fatigue, and poor nutrition.

By March 1839 the sad trek was over. The Cherokees called their journey the "nunna-da-ult-sun-yi," the trail where they cried. The white man has recorded the event as "The Trail of Tears."

Notes

As stated in the "Special Acknowledgments" and "Introduction" sections in the front of the book, many of the speeches, letters, myths, and shamanistic formulas in *Beloved Mother: The Story of Nancy Ward* were adapted from books that contain documented accounts of the originals. Because of the fictional nature of the work, footnotes were not given throughout the text. The adapted material is referred to below by chapter and page number with a reference to where the material can be found in more complete and original form.

Alderman, Pat. *Nancy Ward, Cherokee Chieftainess and Dragging Canoe, Cherokee-Chickamauga War Chief.* Johnson City, Tennessee: The Overmountain Press, 1990.

Ehle, John. *Trail of Tears: The Rise and Fall of the Cherokee Nation.* New York: Doubleday, 1988.

Mooney, James. *Myths of the Cherokee and Sacred Formulas of the Cherokees.* Nashville: Charles and Randy Elder—Booksellers, Publishers, 1982.

Ywahoo, Dhyani. *Voices of our Ancestors: Cherokee Teachings from the Wisdom Fire.* Boston and London: Shambhala, 1987.

1. Chapter 1, pp. 7-8, Lame Deer's petition to the Four Dogs—Mooney, part II, p. 346, "Formula for Treating the Crippler"
2. Chapter 3, pp. 15-16, Long Arrow's narration of the journey—Mooney, part I, pp. 428-429, "Migration Legend"
3. Chapter 3, p. 16-17, Long Arrow's story of the old days when the plants and animals lived as equals with man—Mooney, part I, pp. 250-252, "The Origin of Disease and Medicine"
4. Chapter 4, p. 19, Lone Dove's chant over Tame Doe—Mooney, part II, p. 364, "This Is to Make Children Jump Down"
5. Chapter 5, pp. 27-29, The legends of the Nunnehi—Mooney, part I, pp. 332-337. "The Nunnehi and Other Spirit Folk"
6. Chapter 7, p. 44, The adawehi's proclamation before the ball

play —Mooney, part II, p. 396, "This Concerns the Ball Play"

7. Chapter 7, pp. 46-48, Long Arrow's narration of the Great Ball Play between the birds and animals—Mooney, part I, pp. 286-287, "The Ball Game of the Birds and Animals"

8. Chapter 8, p. 53, The adawehi's formula for going to war—Mooney, part I, p. 388, "What Those Who Have Been to War Did to Help Themselves"

9. Chapter 8, p. 57, Nanyehi's and Kingfisher's departing words to each other—Mooney, part II, p. 376, "Concerning Living Humanity (Love)"

10. Chapter 11, p. 86, Attakullakulla's statement to Colonel Grant—Alderman, p. 21

11. Chapter 13, p. 93, Attakullakulla's message to Henry Stuart—Alderman, pp. 34-35

12. Chapter 14, p. 98, Chief Cornstalk's speech to the Cherokee—Alderman, p. 43

13. Chapter 15, p. 107, Nancy Ward's declaration to the warriors—Alderman, p. 48

14. Chapter 15, pp. 112-114, The stories of the pheasant dance and the groundhog dance—Mooney, part I, pp. 290, 279-280, "The Pheasant Beating Corn: Origin of the Pheasant Dance" and "Origin of the Groundhog Dance: The Groundhog's Head"

15. Chapter 16, pp. 117-118, The Tassel's speech—Alderman, pp. 55-56

16. Chapter 16, pp. 118-119, The soldier's invitation to the Cherokee—Alderman, p. 56

17. Chapter 17, p. 127, The Tassel and John Sevier's exchange—Alderman, p. 64

18. Chapter 17, p. 128, Nancy Ward's speech at the treaty meet—Alderman, p. 65

19. Chapter 19, p. 134, The Tassel's message to Governor Martin—Alderman, p. 67

20. Chapter 19, pp. 135-137, The Treaty of Hopewell, the speech of

the first white commissioner, Chief Tassel's speech, and Nancy
Ward's speech—Alderman, pp. 67-69

21. Chapter 20, pp. 144-145, The Star Woman Myth—Ywahoo, pp.
    29-32
22. Chapter 21, pp. 151-152, Nancy Ward's message to the Cherokee
    Council—Alderman, p. 80
23. Chapter 21, pp. 154-155, The vision of the three Cherokee at
    Oostanaula—Ehle, pp. 97-99
24. Chapter 23, pp. 173-174, The boundaries of Nancy Ward's prop-
    erty—Alderman, p. 81

Resources, Acknowledgments, Suggestions for Further Reading

About Nancy Ward:

Alderman, Pat. *Nancy Ward, Cherokee Chieftainess and Dragging Canoe, Cherokee-Chickamauga War Chief.* Johnson City, Tennessee: The Overmountain Press, 1990.

Clemer, J.D. Scrapbook and newspaper clippings on microfilm at the historical branch of the public library in Cleveland, Tennessee.

Felton, Harold. *Nancy Ward, Cherokee.* New York: Dodd Mead, 1975. This book is a factual account ideal for children ages seven to ten.

Foreman, Carolyn Thomas. *Indian Women Chiefs.* Muskogee, Oklahoma: Star Printery, 1954.

Gridley, Marion E. *American Indian Women.* New York: E. P. Dutton, 1974.

Lillard, Roy G. "The Story of Nancy Ward," *Daughters of the American Revolution Magazine*, January, 1976.

McClary, Ben Harris. "Nancy Ward: The Last Beloved Woman of the Cherokee." *Tennessee Historical Quarterly* 21 (1962): 352-364.

Tucker, Norma. "Nancy Ward, Ghigau of the Cherokee." *Georgia Historical Quarterly* 53: 192-200.

About the Cherokee:

Adair, James. *History of the American Indian.* First published in London, England, 1775. Later reprint is by Blue and Gray Press, Nashville, Tennessee, 1971.

Carter, Samuel. *Cherokee Sunset: A Nation Betrayed: A Narrative of Travail and Triumph, Persecution and Exile.* New York: Doubleday, 1976.

Ehle, John. *Trail of Tears: The Rise and Fall of the Cherokee Nation.* New York: Doubleday, 1988. This book contains the vision of the three Cherokee told at the council meeting in Oostanaula.

Kneberg, Madeline, and Thomas M. N. Lewis. *Tribes That Slumber.* Knoxville: University of Tennessee Press, 1958.

Malone, Henry. *Cherokees of the Old South: A People in Transition.* Athens: University of Georgia Press, 1956.

Mooney, James. *Myths of the Cherokee and Sacred Formulas of the Cherokees.* This book is reprinted by Charles and Randy Elder— Booksellers, Publishers, Nashville, 1982. It contains material collected in field work with the Cherokee Indians from 1887 to 1892. Most of the myths and shamanistic formulas in *Beloved Mother* were adapted from this valuable book.

Perdue, Theda. *The Cherokee.* New York: Chelsea House Publishers, 1989.

Satz, Ronald. *Tennessee's Indian People.* Knoxville, Tennessee: The University of Tennessee Press, 1979.

Starr, Emmet. *History of the Cherokee Indians.* Oklahoma City: The Warden Company, 1921.

Timberlake, Henry. *Memoirs.* London, England, 1765. Reprint by Watauga Press, Johnson City, Tennessee, 1927.

Ywahoo, Dhyani. *Voices of our Ancestors: Cherokee Teachings from the Wisdom Fire.* Boston and London: Shambhala, 1987. This is a beautiful book dealing with the spiritual nature of Cherokee teachings. It is written by a modern Cherokee writer. It is from this book that the myth of Star Woman was adapted for *Beloved Mother.*